BLACK WOLF RISING

ALSO BY A.W. HART

Avenging Angels Series

Concho Series

Gunslinger Series

Legend of the Black Rose Series

BLACK WOLF RISING

CONCHO BOOK EIGHT

A.W. HART

WOLFPACK
PUBLISHING
— EST 2013 —

Text copyright © 2024 A.W. Hart
Special thanks to Eric Beetner for his contribution to this novel.

Published by Wolfpack Publishing
9850 S. Maryland Parkway, Suite A-5 #323
Las Vegas, Nevada 89183

Paperback ISBN 978-1-63977-204-9
eBook ISBN 978-1-63977-415-9
LCCN 2023948991

BLACK WOLF RISING

CHAPTER ONE

HE'D DONE IT TO HIMSELF. NOBODY MADE HIM FOLD HIS SIX foot four frame into the cab of his pickup and sit alone parked under a cottonwood tree, but Concho Ten-Wolves entered hour five of his stakeout feeling the effects of all that time sitting still. His back ached, his leg muscles were starting to cramp, and nothing had happened with the small white house behind the low chain-link fence. Nobody had come or gone, no lights came on in the windows even though it was well past midnight now. The house seemed as deserted as he was told it would be.

But when Alicia Fallen-Tree gave her story to the tribal police about what went on inside the house, Concho believed her. Right then, he was the only one.

Girls were being kept there. A girl, anyway. And she hadn't been the first. They stopped in the vacant house for a day, sometimes two or three, then vanished. They came with escorts. Men with tattoos inked into their skin like graffiti scrawled on a wall. Men with guns hanging from their belts like *caballeros* of old.

Alicia Fallen-Tree's story was checked out, briefly, by the

tribal police, but they found nothing but an empty house. One of many in the dusty landscape of south Texas. One broken window and soon the dry sand and dust would move in, reclaim the property for the land.

But there were no broken windows. No stacks of newspapers on the stoop. No missing roof shingles. For a derelict house, it was in good shape. It gave Concho his first feelings of unease and his first inkling toward believing Maria. On the Rez, people looked out for each other, sure, but they also kept to their own business. A house operating something illegal would have a chance, Concho knew.

He'd spoken to Roberto Echabarri, the sheriff of the tribal police, about it. He was sympathetic to Concho's instinct, but he'd given all the resources he could spare to the claim of a way station for missing girls right there on Kickapoo land and moved his people on to other, more concrete issues.

That left Concho on his own.

He shifted in his seat, the springs groaning under him almost as loudly as his moan of discomfort as he tried to straighten out his back. The two holsters on his hips didn't help him to find a comfortable position, but he was never without his two Colt .45s.

A lone street lamp cast a dim light on the road ahead of him. He'd parked the truck under the cottonwood to avoid the light and stick to the shadows, even if he felt fairly certain nobody was inside the house to see him even if he started up the engine and spun donuts in the street right outside the front door. But he knew protocol, and he liked the discipline of following those rules. A white truck could be easy to see, even at night, when a light source was nearby. A stakeout is all about stealth. He needed to be a viper—covered in natural camouflage but still makes the effort to burrow into the sand to make sure the element of surprise is on its side when the time comes to strike.

The cab of the F-150 still smelled like the burger he'd

eaten hours ago. Concho regretted not getting two. He pulled on the straw in his take-out cup and got nothing back. Empty. Hours in the truck, a large Dr Pepper with no ice meant the cup was empty, but he was full. Nature called and he couldn't put it off much longer.

He tried to distract himself by thinking of what he would say to Alicia. That he'd watched the place and came to the same conclusion as Echabarri? That to post up outside the house for as long as it might take to find out more was beyond his resources as a lone operator? This stakeout was on his own time, not a part of his duties as a Texas Ranger.

He vowed to drive by and keep tabs on the place for the next few weeks. Check in when he could. It was the best he could offer her.

He called a wrap on the stakeout and decided the call of nature couldn't wait until he got home. He opened the door and heard the sounds of the neighborhood at night. Crickets chirped by the dozens. A light desert wind moved the leaves in the cottonwood over his head. Down the block, a dog barked, most likely at one of the night creatures who roamed the neighborhood after midnight. The coyotes, the raccoons, the opossums.

Concho unfolded his long and lean frame from the truck and slowly stretched his muscles to his full height, careful not to move too fast and pull something. He balled both fists and put them in the small of his back and bent his shoulders out over his hips, forcing his spine into a C-shape that felt better and more necessary than relieving himself right then.

He checked around him for any people out late and moved behind the trunk of the cottonwood to unzip his pants.

He let out a deep sigh and then saw the first blink of headlights coming up the block. He moved his whole body behind the tree trunk, embarrassed and not excited about being arrested for public urination, but what had started now, there was no stopping.

As the lights got closer, he could tell it was a pickup. No surprise in a state where the pickup truck is practically the state animal. The brakes squeaked, and the bodywork rattled. From his hiding place behind the tree, he could not see much, but if rust had a sound, this was it.

The truck parked as Concho finished. He zipped up and peered out to see the truck had stopped in front of the empty house. The driver's door opened with a screech of metal, and a man exited. The street light gave his back a yellow tint, and Concho couldn't see enough to make a description stand up in court, but he could tell the man was around five foot ten, wiry, and probably no more than a hundred sixty pounds. He wore cowboy boots and a holster. Again, not a stretch in south Texas and nothing that couldn't ID about two-thirds of the population.

The man moved in front of the truck where his lights were still on, and Concho got a better look as he passed through the pools of light. His skin was tanned like a well-worn saddle. A Mexican or maybe a Kickapoo, like Concho. He looked in his midforties, but it may have been a man a decade younger who had spent too much time in the sun.

He moved through the open chain-link fence and stepped quickly to the front door. Concho watched as the man opened the door with a key and went inside.

Concho tried to move swiftly, but his muscles were still stiff from sitting for so long. He got close enough to the truck to view the license plate. It was a Mexican plate. Three letters, a dash, three numbers, a dash, and one letter. He repeated the combo in his head and moved back to his truck to write it down.

Inside his F-150, he fished a pen and small pad from the glove box. He jotted down the plate number.

After less than two minutes, the front door opened again. This time, the man had a young woman with him. He was walking ahead of her, pulling her along behind him by her elbow. She wore a tank top and a short skirt, barefoot, and seemed to be limping a little. The man tugged at her like she was an untrained puppy. Concho could see that she was crying. Alicia Fallen-Tree had been right. Somewhere inside was a hiding place for that girl and maybe others. His stakeout was over. But Concho Ten-Wolves' night was just beginning.

CHAPTER TWO

THERE WAS A DECISION TO BE MADE, AND CONCHO ONLY HAD seconds to choose. Follow the truck and hope it led him some-place that would explain the mystery girl from the supposedly abandoned house, or bust this guy right here and now.

The decision was made for him when the girl tugged back and tried to rip her arm from the vice grip the man in the boots had on her elbow. The man turned and raised an open hand, poised for a slap. He froze there, something stopping him from following through with the angry impulse. It told Concho someone was waiting for this girl, someone who didn't want her to arrive with a bloody nose or a split lip.

The man lowered his arm and took a step behind her, bringing her arm with him as he went until her wrist and elbow were behind her, then he violently pulled the elbow up. Concho saw the girl buckle, and he heard the involuntary yelp she let out. It looked like he'd dislocated the shoulder, but if he was smart, he'd have come just close enough but not popped the joint out of the socket. If whoever was anticipating this girl cared about her face, they'd care if she had two working arms as well.

The casual violence, the pained scream from the girl, made

up Concho's mind for him. He stepped out of the shadow of the cottonwood tree and began marching across the street toward the rusted-out truck and the vacant house.

The man pushed the girl forward, intent on getting her into the cab of the truck. Once he did, Concho knew she would never be seen again. He didn't know what this involved or who, but this girl's life depended on Concho Ten-Wolves in that moment.

"Texas Ranger, hold it right there."

The .45 had come off his right hip and now rested in a two-handed grip in front of him. His words cut through the night and the nearby crickets all went silent.

The man in the boots tilted his head up to see over the girl. His neck tattoos were nothing but a dark stain in the dim light of the street lamp, but Concho knew gang tattoos when he saw them.

The girl was already in position as a human shield and it gave the man confidence. He drew his gun, keeping his left hand on the girl's elbow.

Concho was already moving. At night, dodging right, he didn't trust his aim to get past the girl so he sought shelter against the side of the pickup. He pressed his shoulder blades into the driver's side door, streaks of cinnamon-colored rust like teardrops down the paint. The engine rumbled in idle and sounded like a wounded animal.

He could hear the man trying to open the passenger side door, but with his gun in one hand and the girl in the other, he hadn't managed it yet. Concho bent down and looked under the truck. He saw their two pairs of legs in a tangle as he tried to muscle her inside.

Concho stood back up, keeping his legs bent so his frame wouldn't poke out above the top of the truck cab.

"Get on the ground. You, the girl, drop to the ground. Now!"

He bent back down to see if she heard him and if she'd obeyed. With a great grunt of pain, she let her body go limp and she slid to the pavement in a heap beside the man's cowboy boots.

Concho spun as he stood and put three bullets through the glass, passing over the seats and out the glass window on the passenger side. He missed but sent the man scrambling.

Concho bent down again and held out a hand to the girl.

"This way!"

She held terror in her eyes when she looked at him. She trusted no man in that moment.

"I'm a Texas Ranger. I'm here to help you."

He hoped his outstretched hand, the pleading in his eyes were enough to convince her. After another moment's hesitation, she began to crawl forward.

Satisfied she was moving, Concho straightened up and peeked over the bed of the truck. He could see the man leap over the short chain-link fence and cower behind it. Not the smartest criminal Concho had ever encountered.

The girl arrived at his feet. He helped her stand, her knees and hands scraped by the street and the gravel.

"That's my truck down there." Concho pointed the way. "Stay low and get there fast. Wait inside and keep your head down. I'll be right there." He pushed her away. "Go!"

She took two stumbling steps before catching herself, then began to run in a crouch toward Concho's F-150.

Concho crept to the back of the truck bed. The back wheel was missing a hubcap. The muffler was tied on with an old coat hanger and the exhaust coming from the tailpipe had a sour, toxic stench to it. He reached the back of the truck where there was no longer a tailgate on the bed. Just deep scrapes in the paint and so many dents it looked like they'd been running a bowling alley out of the back of the truck. His boot scraped against the pavement and gave away his location.

The man stood and fired three quick rounds, piercing the side of his own truck. He let loose a stream of rapid-fire Spanish including some colorful insults Concho had heard only in barrooms and the holding cells after an arrest. Concho had to hunker down and wait out the hailstorm of lead.

This time the man got the door open and he dove across the seat, slicing tiny cuts along his arms from the broken glass on the seats. He sat up behind the wheel and turned his gun over his shoulder and fired one upside-down shot to keep Concho low before dropping the truck in gear.

Concho felt the pickup shift as it went from PARK to DRIVE. He had little choice. Concho swung himself up and into the bed of the pickup truck just as the wheels spun and the truck pulled away from the curb.

The pickup immediately went into a U-turn and Concho slid from one side of the bed to the other, banging his shoulder against the side and adding his own dent to the collection. He nearly lost his .45 but gripped it tighter in his hand. The holster on his left side still held a fresh weapon. Concho got himself on all fours, trying to steady his body as the truck swayed while it picked up speed. As soon as he'd gotten some semblance of balance, the brakes squealed and he lunged forward, smacking his forehead against the back of the truck cab.

The man swung the truck around again in a wild U-turn to now face back the way he'd come, as if he forgot something very important. Must be the girl, Concho thought. He'd realized he couldn't just run away and arrive at whatever meeting he had planned empty-handed.

Concho shook off the knot on his forehead as the truck picked up speed again. He was face to face with a large rust spot. A dark brown ring eaten away entirely in the center. The whole body of the ruck was barely holding on. Concho spun on his backside until his feet were facing the rust spot which was directly behind the driver. He kicked one boot heel at the spot and the rust gave way, opening an eight-inch hole in the metal. Concho rotated to his knees and shoved the .45 into the hole and fired once.

The blast was muffled by being inside the bodywork and by

the back of the seat the barrel was pressed against. But his Double Eagle had power enough to penetrate some stuffing and springs.

The truck veered right and the horn sounded as the man slumped forward, his chest blown out toward the dashboard. Dots of blood spattered the windshield like a red rainstorm inside the cab. Concho held on as the truck went up and over the curb, knocked down a mailbox and then came to a crashing stop against the trunk of a tree two doors down from the abandoned house.

Concho climbed down out of the truck bed as lights came on all around the neighborhood. The Reservation could always be counted on to be quiet at night, especially on a residential street like this one. The hissing of the radiator and the steady blare of the horn broke that silence.

Concho approached the door with his gun at the ready. He slid into view of the window in one smooth move, but there was no return fire. Nothing at all to fear from this man. Concho reached through the broken-out window and pulled the man off the horn and the limp body fell back in the seat. A hole in the man's chest was the same size as the hole he'd kicked in the rusty metal.

Concho holstered his gun and turned to walk back to his own truck where he hoped the girl would still be waiting for him.

CHAPTER THREE

RED AND BLUE LIGHTS FLASHED AND LIT THE NIGHT LIKE A disco. Concho Ten-Wolves stood at the chain-link fence with Roberto Echabarri, the tribal police chief. They looked back toward a police SUV where the girl now sat in the back with a blanket draped over her and a thermos of hot coffee she hadn't touched yet.

"So am I in for some big I-told-you-so?" Echabarri asked. He stood well below Concho, having to tilt his neck to look up at the ranger.

"Alicia Fallen-Tree is a gossip and can't keep a secret, but she isn't a liar."

"We checked it out."

"I know. I just had a gut feeling about it."

Since taking over the job, Concho had been impressed by Echabarri. He had settled in as sheriff nicely and now he seemed genuinely apologetic about missing the truth about the abandoned house.

"She's pretty shaken up," the sheriff said.

"I would think so."

They'd learned her name was Ximena and she had been kidnapped from the Mexico side of the Kickapoo land two days ago. She hadn't given them much to go on, but they hadn't pressed her too hard since she was still in the midst of the trauma of the kidnapping, the violent rescue and the close brush with her own death. They would let her settle before a lengthier questioning.

"I just don't know how we missed it," Echabarri said.

One of his deputies, Araceli Espaderos, one of the few women on the force, stepped from the front door and called to the sheriff and Concho.

"You'll want to see this."

The two men hustled toward the door.

"Hello, Ara," Concho said.

She nodded to him sharply. "Concho. Nice work taking that scumbag down."

"Hope I didn't blow the chance to find out info from him."

She shook her head. "Yeah, that ship has sailed with that hole in his chest."

Echabarri broke in. "What did you want us to see?"

Ara led them into the house and through the living room. She reached the threshold to the large kitchen.

"There was an area rug here and when I moved it, I noticed these grooves in the linoleum."

She pointed to the floor where two half-moon-shaped lines has been scraped into the floor. They made two perfect arcs from the edge of a large chest freezer taking up space against a wall. Ara stepped forward and slid the large, rectangular freezer along the grooves and revealed a trap door cut into the floor.

Echabarri whistled a high note. "Nice work, Ara."

It was a great discovery, but it made Concho wonder how thoroughly they had inspected the property the first time they came out on Alicia Fallen-Tree's report.

Ara bent down and lifted the door by a fat metal ring. A set of wooden steps led down into a dark basement space carved into the crawlspace under the house. She waved a hand, inviting the two men to go ahead.

"Go for it. I've seen it. Don't care to again."

Echabarri gave Concho a look and went first down the steps. Concho had to bend almost in half to make it through the small opening.

Once down in the dungeon, Concho couldn't stand up to his full height. There was a single lightbulb with a pull string. A set of heavy chains bolted to the wall, a dog bowl half full of water and a bucket which explained a lot of the rancid smell down there.

Echabarri held a hand over his nose and mouth and mumbled almost to himself. "This isn't fit for an *anemwa*."

"You're right," Concho said. "Even a dog shouldn't be treated this way."

"This is just a way station. Where was she going after this?"

"That's what I want to know."

"Think she knows?"

"One way to find out."

CHAPTER FOUR

XIMENA SAT IN THE SMALL OFFICE THAT SERVED AS AN interrogation room, storage overflow and where they kept the coffee pot. They didn't do many interrogations on the Rez. Concho knew he would have to involve the Rangers soon, but since this happened on tribal land and he discovered the girl on his own time, not in his capacity as a ranger, he was under no obligation to report it quickly.

Ximena had been given a sweatshirt from the lost and found. A dirty, steel-gray men's large that draped over her like a grease-stained shroud. They had given her a bag of chips, a packet of Hostess cupcakes, and a bottle of water. Only the water had been touched.

Concho watched her through the glass.

"You want this, or should I?" he asked Echabarri.

"Oh, hell no. This is your mess. You deal with it. Sooner I can get this off my books, the better. I'd rather you did this at the ranger station. Hell, I'd rather we turned this whole thing over to the feds. She came across an international border. That's human trafficking right there. I want no part of it. I can't even imagine what the paperwork is going to be on this one."

"So I'm going in alone?"

"I got you a pad and a pen." He held up a yellow legal pad and a ballpoint pen, which Concho took and entered the room with Ximena.

The girl's eyes were still scared of everyone, even the man who had rescued her. He understood.

"Do you have everything you need?"

Ximena nodded and cast her eyes to the floor. She spoke English but haltingly and with little confidence. Concho worried some of her tale would get lost in translation, but since he had nothing at all to explain how she got there and where she might have been headed next, anything she told him would be like a bright light on the investigation.

Concho took the chair opposite her, careful to lift it and not scrape it across the floor. He didn't want any loud noises or sudden moves to spook the girl into silence. She needed to feel safe.

"Is there someone back home we call for you? Let them know you're okay?"

"*Sí. Mi mama y mi padre.*"

Concho nodded his assurance to her. "Okay. We'll do that as soon as I ask you a few questions, okay?"

She nodded.

"Was the man who was with you the same one who took you from your home?"

"No." She had the bottle cap from her water in her hands and she turned in between her fingers. "There were three. *Tres.* They came at night."

"And did you know them?"

"No."

"Never saw them before at all?"

She shook her head.

"Did they tell you where they were taking you?"

"No. They said nothing. They put a bag over my head. Covered my eyes. All I heard was *mi mama* screaming."

Concho made some notes, nodding along to her story.

"Do you know why they took you?"

"I was next, I guess."

"Next?"

"Many girls. They take many girls."

"Who does? Who is they?"

"Cartel."

"They work for a cartel? Drugs?"

She nodded, kept her eyes down and the bottle cap turning.

"Do you know what they had planned for you?"

She nearly shuddered at the thought, then shook her head. "No."

"So you don't know where he was taking you tonight?"

"No. *Lo siento.*"

"You don't have to apologize, Ximena."

He could see a tear fall from her eye and run down the side of her nose then drip off into her lap.

"Did the man say anything that you think could help us understand where you were going? Or do you know what happened to any of the other girls?"

She went rigid, a fear gripping her muscles into knots. She lifted her eyes and as scared as she had been, even in the grasp of the man at the house, Concho saw a deeper fear in her eyes now.

"*El Lobo Negro.*"

"The Black Wolf?"

"*Sí.*"

CHAPTER FIVE

IT DIDN'T TAKE LONG FOR CONCHO TO FIND OUT WHY THE Black Wolf made Ximena so scared.

His real name was Fulgencio Labante, but no one had called him that since his mother died in 1999. He had built a growing and influential drug cartel headquartered on Kickapoo land south of the Rio Grande, but had been busted and had spent the last nine years in a maximum security prison in central Texas.

Before the bust, Fulgencio had established a reputation as one of the more ruthless cartel bosses, choosing violence in nearly every interaction he had with either law enforcement or other cartel leaders. He had rejected any offer to team up or for a buyout from the larger groups in Mexico. His specialty had been ripping out the throats of his enemies to mimic a wolf attack.

The Black Wolf was a mix, just like Concho, only The Black Wolf was half Kickapoo and half Mexican. That's where any similarities between the men ended. The man known as The Black Wolf was the worst kind of criminal. He operated seemingly with no conscience, no rules, no limits to the suffering he would inflict for money and power.

Echabarri came and stood behind Concho where he worked on a computer in the bullpen of the sheriff's station.

"We got word to her parents," the sheriff said. "Hated waking them up but they were damn glad to hear that she was alive and safe."

"She's damn lucky to be alive," Concho said. his eyes still on the computer screen. "You heard of The Black Wolf before?"

Echabarri made a scowl and shook his head. "My father was friends with a Leonard Graywolf, but he died fifteen years ago."

"He is, as they say in the Rangers, a bad hombre. This list of charges is really something."

"And he's behind this?"

"She heard his name, but I don't know how he could be. He's in prison. Has been for nearly a decade."

"Come on, you and I both know it's not impossible for someone to still be a shot-caller from behind bars."

Concho rested his chin on his knuckles. "I guess so." He scrolled down the page of the news report he was reading. "Says here that some said the DEA was tipped off by the Sinaloa cartel. They thought he was getting too big for his britches, plus I don't think they liked a member of the tribe moving in on their territory."

"But he's Mexican."

Concho finally turned away from the screen. "You know how it works. One drop of native blood and they call you an Indian. Same way my African blood tends to override my other half. It confuses people. For the full-blooded Mexicans, they still saw him as an outsider."

"An outsider in his own land. Wonder what that's like?" Echabarri scoffed. "So what next?"

"I don't know. I doubt there's any way to tie this together other than her word, but I wouldn't want to put her through that."

"No," agreed the sheriff. "We should get her home as soon

as we can. Of course ICE wants in on this one. More paper-work," he grumbled to himself.

"I might see what else I can learn, but we might have to take it as a win that we shut down this halfway house, at least."

"You can bet it's not the only one."

"Or if it is, that it can't be replaced in forty-eight hours if they wanted to."

Echabarri rested his hands on his hips. "Quite the life we've chosen for ourselves, isn't it?" Then he yawned.

"Yeah, nothing more we can do about it tonight."

Concho stood and stretched his back.

"Good work, Ten-Wolves," the sheriff said. "You likely saved that girl's life."

"Thank Alicia Fallen-Tree. It was her tip that did it."

Echabarri nodded and ran a hand through his hair.

"I just really want to know what the hell The Black Wolf has to do with this," Concho said.

CHAPTER SIX

THE WALLS OF THE PRISON MESS HALL WERE COLORED A PALE mint green like someone had chosen to paint the cavernous room with toothpaste. The tables and chairs were both a dull steel gray, scarred and dented by years of inmates abusing them. The trays the inmates ate off of were orange, the clothes they wore a pale blue, top and bottom.

The Black Wolf sat in his usual seat. None of the other six hundred and fourteen inmates would dare take his seat. And they all knew better than to call him by his given name. He sat eating his usual double portion of dinner, flanked by his lieutenants. Loyal subjects who would do as he asked and not question an order.

He was medium height, now in his late thirties, though the nine years inside had aged him considerably. He did not partake of the workout routine of many inmates, nor did he bother with a prison job. His belly had gotten round and his muscles small. The fearsome warrior of his youth was gone, but the reputation remained and as long as he lived the life of his moniker, fear would follow him.

He watched a man in line. Short, shaved head, tattoos on each knuckle of both hands.

The Black Wolf believed in stillness. He didn't move unless necessary. He sat perfectly still watching the short man, his own long black hair tied in a ponytail behind him, draping down between his shoulder blades.

His lieutenants kept their eyes on The Black Wolf, waiting for a command. When the short man reached the midway point of the chow line, The Black Wolf nodded so slightly most men would have missed it. The man on either side of him stood and went to the chow line, cutting ahead so they stood directly behind the short man.

The Black Wolf watched.

The short man held out his tray and was served a slopping spoonful of chipped beef in white gravy to go over the slice of white toast already on his tray. The gravy spilled over into the sectioned-off compartment where his green beans were. He frowned but didn't dare complain.

The short man moved on to the dessert. The inmate serving behind the counter gave a quick glance to the two lieutenants standing behind the short man. They gave him a nod.

When the short man held out his tray, the server said, "Sorry, Tommy. I gotta get more from the back. Why dontcha come on back and get it fresh? You'll like it. Chocolate cake with coconut frosting."

Tommy hesitated a moment. He'd never gone behind the counter before, but the server had already walked away from his station and headed into the back kitchen. If Tommy wanted his cake, he needed to follow. And he did.

The two lieutenants set down their trays and followed as well. By the time Tommy noticed them behind him, it was too late to turn back. Tommy stopped and each lieutenant took an elbow and move him forward. The tray fell and chipped beef splattered on the floor like a crime scene.

The Black Wolf watched.

The server inmate who had invited Tommy walked out of the kitchen, back to the chow line with a tray of chocolate cake but didn't stop and didn't look at Tommy as he passed. Waiting inside was a third man who Tommy recognized as one of The Black Wolf's muscle men, Tito.

"Aw, Jesus, Tito. What is this?"

The men on each arm had to hold Tommy up when his knees went weak. Nothing about this could end well for him. Tommy had sixteen more years to go and he never wanted to serve those sixteen more than right then. He'd take the boredom, the repetition, the hopelessness over whatever was about to come.

"Tommy, you know what this is."

"I swear it's not my fault."

Tito held up a hand and Tommy quieted. On the cutting board in front of Tito was a meat cleaver. Tommy's knees gave out again and they had to lift him up.

"Three times you promised." Tito held out three fingers. "Three times."

"I tell you, it's not my fault."

"But, y'see, you brought this to us. To him. You said you could make it happen. And then delay, delay, delay." He ticked off each delay on the three fingers he held up until there were none left, just a fist.

"I know, but what can I do from the inside?"

"You could not make promises you can't keep."

"I'll get it for him, I swear. On Blu-ray. I'll get the whole series. Even the one about the chick, Black Widow, or whatever. I'll make sure he has them all."

"Tommy. Shhh." Tito was the picture of calm. "The Black Wolf, he already has them all. Iron Man, Infinity War, Ant Man. Even the one with the chick. That ain't the point."

Tommy tried to swallow but couldn't. He knew he was going to die here, all over some DVDs of Marvel movies he had foolishly promised to get as a way to earn favor from The Black Wolf. Because in here, if you weren't on The Black Wolf's side, you were his enemy. And his enemies didn't last long. But to die over some superhero movies...Tommy regretted even thinking his lazy sister would come through for him. And what a stupid thing to die for.

"Please, Tito. Please. I don't wanna die."

"No, no, no. Relax, Tommy. Relax. You're not gonna die here today." He held up three fingers again. "But three times? Breaking a promise three times, Tommy? That's no good. That won't do. We can't have it."

"I get it. I hear you. I know."

"I know you know. But in case you ever forget." Tito dropped his three fingers again and a shocking thought hit Tommy. Tito picked up the cleaver. "We're gonna make sure and give you a reminder to carry with you."

The two lieutenants shoved Tommy forward. He fought back and tried to squeeze out of their grip. He shouted, begging harder than he would have if it had been his life he was convinced he was about to lose, and not just his fingers.

"No, Tito, no! Please, you can't. I promise they'll be here next week. I never meant to break a promise to him. It's not my fault. It's not my fault!"

The door to the kitchen swung open and a guard stood there, a rifle in his arms pointed at the ground.

"Hey!" the guard said, giving the men a hard stare.

Tommy went quiet and all eyes turned to the guard.

"Keep it down, for Christ's sake, okay? And get on with it. This is taking too long."

The guard ducked back out the door. Tommy began whimpering and they forced his right hand down onto the cutting board.

The Black Wolf brought a fork full of cake to his mouth, his eyes never wavering from the kitchen door. He waited for the delicious sound of Tommy's scream.

A guard at the back of the room stepped away from his position against the wall, keeping a wide eye on the room full of inmates, and stepped to The Black Wolf's table.

He bent slightly, tilting closer to the man sitting still except for a slight working of his jaw as he chewed.

"There's a problem with the girl," the guard said.

Without turning, The Black Wolf lifted a hand, silencing the guard.

"Not now. Later."

"I just wanted you to know. James Lee said there was an issue."

"Later," he said again, then dropped his hand.

A moment later came the scream. All chatter stopped in the room. The inmates all around him made a point not to look at the kitchen or at The Black Wolf. They were determinedly ignoring the scream and then the next.

The room slowly went back to its normal chatter, the scraping of forks against the plastic trays, the clack of aluminum cups against the steel table tops.

Tommy screamed a third time. Nobody acknowledged it except for The Black Wolf who let a slight grin lift the left side of his mouth. He fed himself another bite of cake.

Tito came out of the swinging kitchen door alone. None of the other inmates looked his way, nor did the guards. Tito reached The Black Wolf and unfolded a napkin in his hand and dumped three of Tommy's fingers onto the tray.

The Black Wolf gave a slight dip of his chin and speared the last bite of cake with his fork. Before he ate it, he said, "Another." Tito went off quickly to get his boss another slice of cake.

CHAPTER SEVEN

CONCHO RAN DOWN ALL HE KNEW TO DALTON SHAW, commander of the Texas Rangers company D and Concho's boss, but Shaw knew most of it already, having read the report.

"So this is what you do with your time off?" Shaw asked Concho.

"Not usually, no."

Shaw flipped through the pages of the report and then shut the file folder. "Not much to go on. Kind of a dead end from here, huh?"

"Well, I wanted to talk to you about that, sir."

"I get the sense you're about to ask me for a favor, Ten-Wolves."

"Yes, Chief, I am."

"And you think you've earned this favor?"

"That'll be for you to decide. But this isn't an isolated incident. Ximena wasn't the first girl taken across the border."

"First one I've heard about," Shaw cut in.

"I know, sir. But that might be because she was taken off the Rez in Mexico. There's a different standard of reporting there."

"Meaning they keep to themselves," he said. Concho

nodded. "Not too different from what I've seen out in Eagle Pass."

"If there's an issue on tribal lands that doesn't need to involve the Rangers, most people figure it shouldn't."

Shaw nodded his understanding. "Go on. Ask away."

"I'd like to follow up on this. Make it my priority for a few days. A week, maybe. Let me see what I can find out and if I come up blank, I'll drop it. For now."

Shaw sighed. He steepled his fingers under his chin. Shaw's jacket was slung over the back of his chair and his white shirt strained against his muscled chest and arms. His plain black tie was cinched all the way to his buttoned collar. By the book all the way. His hat hung on a hook behind him, only an arm's reach away. An essential part of the ranger uniform to Dalton Shaw. Concho had once again left his hat behind, his straight black hair uncovered and flashing his Kickapoo heritage for all to see.

"I remember that Black Wolf bust," Shaw said. "Big deal at the time. Rangers dined out on a bust like that for weeks, even if the feds took most of the credit for it."

"Do you recall who the arresting officer was?"

"I certainly do. Jack Bennett. Good Ranger. Would have fit in with the job in the 1800s just as well. Hardscrabble guy, tough as leather."

"Do you know which office he works out of?"

"Retired now. He rode that bust into the sunset. Hell of a way to go out."

Concho committed the name to memory. Jack Bennett.

"Well, chief, what do you think?"

Shaw exhaled again and tapped his finger on his desk blotter. "We have a protest at the new border wall that I was requested to give some support to. Those Border Patrol softies always need our help with something, it seems." He eyeballed Concho up and down. "But I guess I can spare you from that. You want a week?"

"Maybe less."

"Let's shoot for that. Okay, Ten-Wolves. You check it out. If someone's bringing girls into my territory and doing Lord knows what with them, and if this Black Wolf is involved somehow, I want to know about it. Anything you learn comes straight back to me, got it?"

"Yes, Chief."

"Okay then. Dismissed."

Concho stood. "One more thing."

"Don't push it, Concho."

"I won't, sir. The girl. Is she scheduled to go back home yet?"

Shaw shook his head. "ICE hasn't released her yet. You know those federals. Paperwork and bureaucracy will probably last a month or more."

"And where is she?"

"In our custody. We've got her safe and sound. She doesn't need to be off in some ICE facility with no blankets and one-ply toilet paper."

Concho tucked his hands into his front pockets. "Well then, sir. I guess I have one more favor to ask."

CHAPTER EIGHT

MARIA MORALES WAS WAITING FOR CONCHO WHEN HE ARRIVED home. She didn't expect the other woman who followed her boyfriend in.

"I can explain," he said.

"If the words three-way come out of your mouth," she said, "I'm leaving you."

Concho held up his hands. "No, no. Nothing like that. This is Ximena."

He introduced the girl to Maria. They stood eye-to-eye at the same five-foot-four. Maria's hair was longer but both women wore it straight. They could have been cousins.

Concho explained as concisely as he could the situation, and how Chief Shaw had allowed Ximena to stay with them until she was cleared to return to her family in Mexico.

"I should've asked first," he said.

"Yes, you should have." Maria looked at the frightened girl. "But I get it." She waved Ximena inside. "Welcome. *Mi casa es su casa.*"

Ximena smiled a weak grin. "*Gracias.*"

"*Agua?*" Maria asked.

Ximena nodded.

Maria flicked her head to indicate she wanted Concho to follow her into the kitchen. He did, expecting an earful for his presumptuous decision.

"Not exactly the greeting I was expecting, Concho."

"I know, I'm sorry."

"I was kind of hoping to show you how much I missed you last night."

He got the hint and felt bad he had missed the opportunity. "It won't be for long." He knew that might not be true. ICE processing could be a notoriously slow ordeal. He pulled her into a hug, wrapping her in his arms and folding her into his body. He leaned down and kissed her. She opened her mouth to him and let him know how much he had been missed. When they broke the kiss, he said, "Do you mind keeping an eye on her while I go check out a lead?"

Maria cocked a hip to one side. "I didn't sign up to be a babysitter."

"I know, I know. I just need to move quickly with this. Shaw is only giving me a few days. She won't be any trouble. Let her watch TV or something. She's been through a lot."

Maria turned and looked at the girl sitting on the couch, her hands folded in her lap.

"I can't imagine."

"So you'll be okay while I'm out?"

She playfully punched him in the stomach. "Go. But be back soon."

"Thank you." He kissed her quickly, grabbed an apple off the counter and headed out.

* * *

JACK BENNETT LIVED IN A CLASSIC RANCH-STYLE HOME WITH A sign lettered in wood-burned letters, COYOTE FLAT.

The spread ran far off to the east with a small pond, a barn and a paddock where Concho counted two goats, three sheep, and a mule. He parked his truck and stepped out into a light wind that carried a mixture of smells from the livestock and a healthy bed of wildflowers along the side of the house.

Concho knocked on the front door.

"C'mon in!" a voice called from inside. Concho pulled open the screen door and entered. The house was done in leather and dark wood. Longhorns hung on at least three walls that he could count, mule deer heads on two others and a stuffed owl in flight hung over the leather sofa.

Jack Bennett sat in a leather recliner. He waved Concho in. He was a silver-haired man, hard to tell how tall from his seated position, but a barrel-chested man whose gut had gone wide in his retirement. No way a physique like that would fly in the Rangers, but after years of keeping in top shape for the uniform, Bennett had clearly been enjoying his twilight years.

"You must be the one they call Concho," Jack said.

"Yes, Mr. Bennett. Good to meet you."

Concho shook his outstretched hand.

"Aw, call me Jack. Ain't no formalities between Rangers." His accent was dry and Texan as a tumbleweed.

"Thanks for seeing me on short notice."

"No problem. Pardon my not getting up. Back's been acting up again lately. Don't like to move it if I don't have to. These spells can last a few days sometimes."

"Sorry to hear it."

"Downside of the job. I put my body through hell. Only thing I can say is I never caught a bullet."

"Well, that's good news."

Jack pointed to the sofa. "Have a seat. Got a pitcher of iced tea if you like some. Good beer in the fridge too, you're welcome to it."

"Tea is fine. Thank you." As Concho poured himself a glass, he started in with what he wanted to know. "So you brought down The Black Wolf?"

"Yeah, Shaw said you wanted to talk about that." He laughed at the memory. "Nasty son-of-a-gun, that one. Probably the best bust of my career. Brought him in, killed five of his guys, took in six million bucks worth of cocaine, three hundred eighty grand in cash, twenty-six assault rifles and a box of hand grenades. Made quite the photo op. You know how they like to parade the contraband."

"Yes, sir, I do. Can I top you off?" Concho poured more tea into Jack's glass. "So the reason I ask is that a girl turned up in some halfway point between Mexico and some spot up north. We rescued her and the only thing she could tell us about why she was taken was the name The Black Wolf. I was hoping you might shed a little light on this for me."

"This was recently?"

"Night before last."

Jack scratched at his chin where he hadn't shaved in a while. "You think she was going to see him?"

"She doesn't know who he is. If she was being taken to him, that strikes me as odd seeing as he's still in prison."

"And that's where he'll be 'til his dying day. I made damn sure of that."

"Do you think he could still have any influence over his old business?"

Jack took a sip of tea and smiled. "That wouldn't surprise me a bit. Lots of these guys can still run things from behind bars. See, nobody wants to be the top dog. Top man in a Mexican cartel is a job with a very low life expectancy. Someone is always gunning for you. So the second and third in command are glad to let someone else be the man while they still get the money, but with less risk." He got a grin on his face. "It's like no one wants to be on top of the totem pole, and no one wants to be on the bottom either. Right in the middle, that's the sweet spot, right? I don't know how it is for you people. You probably want to be on the top."

"Totem poles are actually from the Pacific Northwest. People like the Tlingit and Haida and Canadian First Nations people. We don't have those down here with *my people*."

Concho took a deliberate sip of his tea and gave Jack a

hard look. He didn't think the old man meant any harm, but he didn't want him to go uncorrected.

"And who are your people, exactly? You got a face like every other NBA player I ever seen, but you got that big chief hair and that running brave attitude. So which is it? Me, it makes no never mind. I think a man ought to be proud of who he is and where he come from, not matter where that is. But you don't look like you can make up your mind."

"Little bit of both," Concho said. He kept a steady gaze on the man, trying to decide if he was out of date or an old-school racist like too many Rangers of the past. "You want to share opinions about slaves picking cotton and I have thoughts on that too. Very little cotton being picked in Texas back in the day. But the totem pole thing, that rubs me a little bit since those tribes are so far away it might as well be another country. Like asking a German for a good recipe for Lasagna."

"Still," Jack said, losing his smile. "You get my point."

"So he could still be calling shots from behind bars."

"Could be. The Black Wolf wasn't eager to give up power."

"Did he move girls across the border before?"

"He was into all kinds of nastiness if he could make a buck. He could have, maybe not. Hell, not a damn thing would surprise me with that man, though."

Concho could see he wasn't going to get anything concrete from Bennett, but it was a step in the right direction. Concho looked around the room, trying not to feel the owl looming over his head. He spotted a photo of a younger, slimmer Jack with a wide smile in a handshake with a man in a ranger dress uniform handing Jack a medal. Next to the photo was a shadow box with the medal in it on a silk ribbon.

Concho stood and walked to the photo. "Medal of valor?"

"You betcha. For that same bust we're talking about. Figured that was cue to exit stage left, as they say. Weren't gonna get no better than that. I was ready for retirement anyhow."

"And how's it been? Nice spread you got here."

"It'd be better if my wife was still alive to enjoy it with me. All I got was one year with her and me not traipsing off at all hours putting myself in the crosshairs. She's the reason I have that damn mule and them goats out there. Only animal I need is a good dog."

"Animals are good for us. Keep us connected to the land."

"If you say so. Damn needy and stubborn. Mule's already got that reputation, but them goats and sheep are just as bad."

"No horses?"

"Ranger pension only pays for so much. I wanted a black stallion. Got a mule instead."

Concho walked back to the sofa. "Well, thanks for meeting with me. I appreciate your time."

"No problemo. You really think The Black Wolf is up to his old tricks again?"

"He's in this somehow. I just need to know how so I can keep any other girls from being snatched."

"Hell, I'd come out of retirement tomorrow if it meant I could bust that man again."

Concho set down his glass of iced tea. "You call me if you think of anything that might help."

"Will do."

They shook hands.

"Hey, Ranger," Jack said. "You keep fightin' the good fight."

"Will do."

Concho walked back toward the front door.

"One riot, one ranger," Jack called after him.

"Yes, sir."

The screen door slapped shut behind him.

CHAPTER NINE

Concho kept the truck at a steady fifty-five miles per hour on the way back to Eagle Pass giving him time to go over what he knew so far, but in truth there was little to think about. He needed to convince himself to be satisfied that he'd rescued Ximena and be done with it. But the nagging thought that this was a cycle that would pick up again and the next girl may not be so lucky kept at him, wearing him down. He knew Maria would be expecting him home, but he needed to stop off at the abandoned house again, look for anything he might have missed.

Concho entered the boundaries of the Rez and steered away from his own home and toward the residential street that had only a few days before been interrupted by gunfire and death.

He parked under the same cottonwood tree, scanning the street for anyone else who might be watching the house. The neighbors were all closed up, doors shut, blinds drawn. He approached the house with its slashes of yellow crime scene tape. One end had already come loose and flapped in the light breeze. The sun had started to dip down to the horizon. Night would come quickly now. Concho felt the same way about this case, that darkness was coming on fast and soon there would be nothing to see.

He walked up the path and tore down the crime scene tape, balling it in his fist and entering the front door. He tossed the wadded-up ball of yellow tape into the corner. No sense keeping things clean. Now that people were paying attention to the house, if no legal owner could be found, it would be turned over to the tribal council and either sold or auctioned off soon. Perhaps some family could make a home from this house of horrors again.

He didn't want to go back down to the basement dungeon again if he didn't have to, and that was the area that had gotten the most scrutiny before. Surely nothing was missed there. He'd never been upstairs so Concho mounted the staircase. He thought how disturbing it was that whoever these men were had used the Kickapoo lands as both their hunting ground and their storage facility. How someone with native blood could exploit their own people bothered him more than if a white man had done it.

Dust coated the floor in the upstairs hall. It obviously hadn't been used for anything in quite a long time. No answers to be found there either.

Concho heard a noise from downstairs. Sounded like the door opening. He stopped and tilted an ear toward the railing. He heard footsteps, then a man's voice.

"Ricky? *Dónde estás?*"

They had ID'd the man Concho shot as a Ricardo, so he assumed that was the Ricky this man was now looking for.

"Yo, Ricky!"

Concho peered down the steps and, seeing it clear, descended as quietly as he could. He decided not to start out antagonizing so he kept the Colt .45s in their holsters. For now.

He reached the base of the stairs and heard the man in the kitchen. Concho stood square facing that direction before he spoke. "Can I help you?"

The man quickly jerked his head around and froze when

he saw Concho. He stood about six foot, dark hair, tanned skin. He wore a flannel work shirt, jeans, boots, in need of a shave. He would pass unnoticed in any town in Texas from the panhandle to the border.

"*Inglés?*" Concho asked.

"Who the hell are you?" the man said in a heavy accent. But he understood.

"Well, I'm not Ricky. So we got that out of the way, why don't you tell me who you are?"

The man squinted a little, trying to figure if Concho was a threat or not. The upside to Concho's stanch refusal to regularly wear his badge or his ranger hat was that people didn't automatically flag him as law enforcement. But his six-foot-plus frame and the two Colts on his hip made him a threat to almost anyone. The man decided he was a threat, or at least he had a long way to go to earn this man's trust. He squared up against Concho, backlit by the kitchen light, shadows falling over his face making it hard for Concho to read his expression.

"I'm Óscar. You looking for Ricky too?"

"No, I found him already." Concho let Óscar wonder over what that meant. "You, uh, looking for anyone else around here?" Concho let his eyes cut over to the chest freezer, letting Óscar know he knew what was under there.

"Is Ricky coming back?"

"I doubt it."

Óscar took a few steps forward. "You tell him I was here, eh? You tell him I was looking for him."

"That mean you're leaving?"

Concho blocked his path to the door and Óscar looked for a way around the tall man that would avoid a fight.

"No, Ricky, no reason for me to be here," Óscar said.

"Why don't you hold on there, Óscar. I got a few more questions for you."

A flash of understanding came over Óscar's face. "*Los Diablos Tejanos*," he said, referring to the nickname the Rangers had among criminals south of the border. The Texan Devils.

"We prefer Rangers, if you don't mind."

Óscar made his move. He rushed forward, dipping a hand behind his back for the gun hidden there tucked into his belt. Concho watched him coming a mile away. He drew with his right hand and put his left hand on Óscar's wrist at his back, freezing the man's gun arm in place. They were nose to nose now, coming together quickly. Concho's .45 was pressed to Óscar's forehead between his eyes. They paused there for a breath, then Óscar stabbed his left hand across him and made a grab for Honcho's other Colt. With one hand occupied keeping Óscar's gun safely tucked away, Concho had no choice but to use his gun hand to reach down and clamp onto the other wrist to keep his own gun in its holster.

They stood in a tangled stand-off, inches apart, hands on hands, guns tucked away. Óscar tugged at both arms, trying to free one of the guns, it didn't matter which. Concho started to sweat with the effort of holding the other man in place. His grip on the Colt in his right hand started to slip.

Neither man spoke. Óscar made little grunts of effort as he pulled at his arms. They shifted on their feet, tiny steps like a dance in a pirouette through the center of the room until they ended up with Óscar's back to the front door.

Concho knew he would have to release one hand. He didn't want to shoot this man. He wanted to question him. Ask about *El Lobo Negro* and the girl and if there were more girls coming. But if he let go and allowed Óscar to draw on him, he would have no choice.

Concho let the .45 in his hand fall to the floor. He could barely keep hold of Óscar's wrist with it filling his palm. He kicked at it with the heel of his boot, sending the gun off into the baseboard. He pulled up on the arm reaching around Óscar's back.

Óscar's arm came out holding his gun, a black .38 revolver. Concho still had a firm grip on his wrist and he held it out to the side, keeping the barrel far away from his body. He shoved forward, driving the two of them toward the doorway to the kitchen. He slammed Óscar's wrist into the door jamb. Óscar cried out, but held tight to the gun.

The Mexican twisted his body, threw up knees and tried to hit Concho in the groin. He grunted and gritted his teeth, a wild animal trapped and cornered. Concho tried to use his leverage to keep Óscar in his control. He banged the man's wrist against the doorway again. Óscar cried out in pain, but the gun stayed in place.

Concho felt Óscar's boots on his own feet and ankles as the man tried to sweep his legs out from under him, but they were too close together and locked in their grip for it to do much good.

All the while, Óscar pulled on Honcho's other .45, lifting it an inch from the holster before Concho forced it back down. Sweat beaded on his forehead and his breathing became labored. This grappling held his muscles in a tight knot and the first man to break would lose the battle for the guns.

One more time Concho slammed Óscar's wrist into the doorway and finally the gun fell away. In the moment of surprise and pain, Concho pitched his head forward and head-butted Óscar into a gush of blood from his nose. Óscar leaned back, too late to pull away from the powerful blow, but the way the men were tangled he pulled Concho down on top of him.

They hit the linoleum floor of the kitchen in a pile, Óscar taking the worst of it as Concho flopped on top of him. The second .45 skittered away and crashed to a stop against the chest freezer. Concho rolled off, desperate not to lose control of the gun. He crawled on all fours across the greasy floor toward his Colt.

Óscar was up and running, one hand to his face and leaking blood between his fingers and spewing a string of profanities in Spanish. He half ran-half stumbled toward the front door, veering right at the last second when his eye lit on his prize.

Concho fit his gun back into his grip and turned in time to see Óscar lean over and reach for the twin .45 laying against the baseboard in the living room. Concho fired once. A hole opened up in the plaster next to Óscar's head, spraying him with dust and wood splinters.

He recoiled and skidded his way toward the door.

Concho fired again and the bullet punched the door, but missed Óscar. From his position on the floor, his aim was reduced to rookie level. Óscar tore open the door and didn't look back as he leaped out into fresh air. Concho fired one more round to chase him out the door, but it stuck in the doorframe.

Concho took a moment to unfold his long legs and maneuver himself to standing. He took the living room in four long strides, but by the time he reached the door he saw Óscar's truck pulling away, the driver's side door swinging open as Óscar hadn't bothered to waste time shutting it behind him.

Since Concho had parked his own truck halfway down the block, he knew it would be useless to give chase.

Word would get back now. The girl was gone, and so was Ricky. The Black Wolf, or whoever was working on his behalf, would know the house was compromised. No more girls would be coming through here. But Concho knew it wasn't over. They would move to another house. They would pause for a few days, a week maybe, then start up again.

Concho Ten-Wolves wasn't about to let that happen.

CHAPTER TEN

JAMES LEE MORRIS HAD HEARD ENOUGH WHINING. THE narrow confines of the trailer home seemed to press every syllable of the tearful, high-pitched pleading and crying from the man being held down on the sofa in front of him. They called the man Spider, James Lee assumed because of the lopsided spider web tattoo on his chest, but he had no idea if the nickname had come first or the ink. He honestly didn't give a damn.

Spider wore only a dirty pair of jockey shorts and he was skinny as a rail. Two men held him to the couch, but it would have only taken one. James Lee liked to be prepared, though. And if he told the truth, he liked having sidekicks. It felt good to snap his fingers and have men who spent four to five hours a day in the gym do whatever he asked of them.

Of course, James Lee had to respond to the snap of The Black Wolf, but he enjoyed serving as the outside presence of a man so feared. James Lee carried the shadow of The Black Wolf with him into any room he entered. People knew he was the right hand of the big boss behind bars. Whatever James Lee said might as well have come from the lips of The Black Wolf himself.

The errand today at Spider's trailer was a small thing, one James Lee didn't bother the boss man with. Cleaning up accounts, is all.

He raised a hand, trying to get the screeching whine to stop. When Spider kept right on going, he nodded to the side-kicks. The one on the right balled a fist and James Lee saw the biceps bulging from the sleeve of his black T-shirt flex and pulsate the red rose tattooed there before he cut a right cross to Spider's nose.

Finally, the sad excuses stopped.

The only sound in the trailer now was a low whimper from Spider and the sound of a horsefly trapped inside and banging brainlessly against a screen to get out, as if it might be next for James Lee's wrath.

"That's a whole lotta talk all to say 'I ain't got it,' Spider."

"I know, I know, but…" He snorted up a clot of blood from his newly broken nose. "I'm tellin' you my guy ran off and I ain't heard from him in near a week."

"So you hire dumber-than-rocks junkies to deal your product on the street, then they run off with the goods, and you somehow think that matters a flea's testicle to me? You got to employ better hiring practices, Spider."

James Lee leaned back in the rickety chair, his only option for seating besides sitting next to Spider on the sofa, but that looked so stained with questionable spots that James Lee would rather have licked the floor of a truck stop bathroom. He wore his usual Western shirt with pearl buttons. A bolo tie with a turquoise clip. Black jeans, a silver belt buckle with the state of Texas embossed on it. He didn't have the muscles of his side-kicks, nor did he need them. James Lee held a peculiar dead-eyed look that gave people a shiver when they looked at him. He could frighten a rabid coyote with one look. Something about the flat, black dullness behind his eyes let you know this was a man with no moral compass and no bottom to his depravity. The Black Wolf hired him after getting to know him as a guard. He was one of the first to take a payoff from The

Black Wolf, and he'd proved a loyal soldier. When he came to
The Black Wolf offering to work for him full time, the boss
knew the advantages of having someone from the area, a white
man, a former guard, and a man who would burn his own
childhood home to the ground for money. Really, it had been
his eyes. The Black Wolf had seen those eyes and knew this was
a man he wanted to work for him. Being on the other side of
those dead eyes was not an option. Keep this man close, or live
in fear.

He let loose a sigh.

"Don't think I don't get the irony here. Obviously our
employment skills were lacking when we brought you on. But,
in all fairness now, we didn't approve you sub-contracting out
the selling of the product we provided, did we?"

"Well, no but—"

James Lee held up a hand again to silence him. This time
he listened.

"I know the answer to that already. It's what they call
rhetorical. That's your vocabulary word for the day. The question is what are we gonna do about this now? If I have to
expend resources to go find this fool you trusted, and I may
never find him at all, then that's just throwing good money
after bad. And it's taking on something that ain't my responsibility. So—"

His cell phone rumbled in his pocket, derailing his train of
thought.

"Spider, I ought to—"

The phone went again and James Lee knew he wouldn't
get to finish his thought unless he took the call. He stood and
wedged the phone from the front pocket of his very tight jeans.
He checked the screen and decided it was worth taking. He
waved to his two friends who followed him outside.

"Right back," he said to Spider.

On the cinder block being used as a front step, he pointed
to a shovel in the dirt yard in front of the trailer and snapped
his fingers. The same sidekick who had punched Spider got the

shovel and shoved the handle through the grip on the door to the trailer, sealing Spider inside in case he got any ideas to run. The other sidekick went around the side without being asked to keep an eye on the one tiny window Spider might be capable of crawling out of.

James Lee answered his phone.

* * *

ÓSCAR KEPT HIS HEAD LEANED BACK. THE SOCK FULL OF ICE was wet now and didn't sit firmly across the bridge of his nose.

"We got a problem," he said. The words came out muffled through the two wads of paper towel he had stuffed up his nostrils.

"Not my favorite way to start on conversation," James Lee replied.

"Ricky's gone and so is the girl. There was some guy there."

"What guy?"

Óscar was reluctant to say. A conversation with James Lee on the best day was stressful and unsettling, but delivering bad news…well, there was a reason he called him and chose not to see him in person.

"A ranger."

He heard James Lee let out a long exhale into the phone.

"So Ricky was busted or what?"

"Not sure. Just gone. We didn't get into details before he started shooting at me and busted my damn nose."

"Did you check the basement?"

"Didn't have time."

"So she could have still been there? Maybe Ricky got busted and never made it there to get her. You think about that?"

"I guess maybe, but I doubt it. He sure acted like he knew what was up. *El diablo*."

"No, Óscar," James Lee said. "The devil wouldn't have let

you live."

If anyone knew about such things, James Lee would, Óscar thought.

"So what do I do?"

"See if you can find out what they know and if Ricky is with them."

"Okay. I'll try."

"Don't make me go Yoda on you."

"Okay, okay. I won't try. I'll do it."

"*Bueno.*"

* * *

JAMES LEE HUNG UP AND TURNED BACK TO THE TRAILER. THIS news had taken all the momentum from his visit with Spider. Nothing would come from trying to reason with this man. He could tell by looking at his skinny frame and dirty hair that the kid was using the product. He most likely was blaming some phantom dealer friend for running off with stuff he used himself. Not worth the trouble or the breath it would take to get the truth.

He had bad news to deliver to The Black Wolf.

James Lee waved a finger at the side of the trailer and slumped away like a bored teenager. The sidekicks got the command from that simple gesture. One walked to the propane tank that fed the trailer and gripped the knob. With a flex of his massive arm muscles, he tore it clean off. A sulfur smell and slow hiss filled the air.

The other sidekick had gathered a dead bush from the yard. He took the dry, brown sticks and lit it with a Zippo from his pocket. He laid the burning bush along the side of the trailer and walked away.

James Lee let them open the door for him to the back seat of their Lincoln Navigator. They hadn't gotten more than a hundred yards away when the tank blew and Spider was no more.

CHAPTER ELEVEN

Concho had already apologized three times for not having a guest room and making Ximena sleep on the couch. The woman kept batting away his apologies and thanking him for not having to sleep at an ICE detention facility.

He had also apologized to Maria for being gone so long and leaving her to look after Ximena. As they were seated together at the small square table off the kitchen he said he was sorry one more time.

"It's okay," Maria said. "I'm keeping track of the hours and you are gonna owe me *big time* by the end of this." She smiled and leaned over to kiss the tip of his nose.

"I'll check and see if they have any word when she'll be released to go back to her family."

"I hope it's soon, and not for me, but for her sake. I can't imagine what she's been through. All I'd want is to be close to the people I love if I'd survived something like that."

"I know what you mean."

Ximena stood in the small kitchen nook making fried eggs and chorizo. She had insisted on making breakfast for them as a way to say thank you.

Maria gave Concho a lifted-eyebrow look. "If her cooking is better than mine, you keep it to yourself."

He smiled and nodded.

"So, are you gonna be okay if I head in and talk to Shaw? I can't stick around and watch her if I'm on a timetable to get this thing figured out. If I run out this week and have nothing to show for it, they'll close up this case like that shoe store at the mall that went out of business."

"I guess I can take her with me to the mall. Plenty to do there. I can't give her work to do or anything, but she can hang out in the food court or sit by the fountain."

"That would be amazing. Thank you."

"Let me just mark down yet another favor." She made a mark in an invisible notebook and gave him a sly smile. "You're running quite the tab, Mr. Ten-Wolves."

"I always pay my debts, ma'am."

"Good thing for you, we accept all kinds of currency."

She squeezed a hand on his thigh. From the kitchen, Ximena said, "*El desayuno es listo.*" Breakfast was ready.

* * *

CONCHO DROVE INTO RANGER HQ IN WESLACO AND RAN DOWN for Dalton Shaw what had happened at the house the night before. Shaw listened with a worried knot on his brow.

"You are sure you don't want anyone else on this with you?" he asked. "Not that I have a single body to spare right now."

"No," Concho said. "It's slow going. I doubt anyone will come back to the house after that. They know it's burned as a location. The question is, where is the plan B house?"

"Could be close, could be a hundred miles from here."

"I know. If the girls are coming off the Rez on the Mexico side, chances are good they'll want to stick to a spot on the Rez up north, but if they're smart, they'll either lay low for a while or move far away."

"And if this has been going on for a long time and we just found out now, then they're smart, all right."

"That's a nasty combination right there. Smart, ruthless, and rich."

"That's a cartel for you."

Concho felt good to be on the same page as Shaw on this one. He knew the clock was ticking on Shaw's patience, but for now, his commander was still on his side in wanting to see a solution, and to prevent it from happening again in their jurisdiction.

"I think I want to go and check out what's going on where they're keeping The Black Wolf."

"Which unit is he at?"

"William Wallace unit."

"Bigfoot? Damn. That's for the worst of the worst."

Concho nodded. "Maybe I can find out some more if I talk to the warden."

Shaw tapped some keys on his computer, pulling up a map of the Texas prison system.

"Damn, Concho, that's two hundred miles north."

"I know. It's a big ask."

Shaw leveled a stare at Concho over the top of his computer monitor. "Seems like all you got these days are big asks." Concho gave him back a slight shrug and his most apologetic look, which didn't come off as very sincere.

"Not much more to be learned down here. I figure it's time to go to the source."

"Hold on." Shaw typed some more on his keyboard. "Right. I thought so." He tapped a finger against the screen. "This came in a few days ago. I didn't think I had the resources for it, but maybe this is perfect timing."

Concho stood and moved around Shaw's desk to look at the email he had pulled up.

"From the marshals," Shaw said, summarizing the request. "They're looking to serve a warrant on a guy. Native American. Not Kickapoo, I don't think, but still. They were asking the Rangers help to see if we had anyone who could get them in close. Seems they've had trouble with this fella in the past getting tipped early. Kind of a tight-knit group, if you know what I mean."

Concho let that one go.

Shaw tapped the screen again. "But it's up around that neck of the woods. I could send you up there in the line of duty and look good for the marshals, then you could go take care of business at the prison."

"Tailor made."

"Let me make a few calls, see if they already got someone."

Concho gave him a dubious look. "Rangers hire on more Native Americans while I wasn't looking?"

CHAPTER TWELVE

CONCHO LEFT A NOTE FOR MARIA. HE KNEW THERE WOULD BE a lot of explaining to do when he got back, but he figured delaying Maria's anger at him a few days wasn't a bad thing.

As he turned his truck toward the highway north, though, he had second thoughts. With a deep sigh, Concho turned the truck toward Highway 375 and the Mall de las Aguilas.

He parked and made his way past the open stores toward Maria's office where she oversaw the mall and both its retailers and shoppers. He saw her bent over her desk, her long ponytail falling over one shoulder. He felt a surge of adrenaline. He still found her very attractive and she was never sexier than when she was in business mode.

Maria felt his stare and looked up, smiling when she saw him.

"May I help you, sir?"

"Just wanted to see the brains of the operation."

Maria leaned back in her chair, pushed out her chest so he could see. "Is that all I am to you? A set of brains?"

"Not at all, Miss Morales. Not at all."

She set down her pen and stood. "Why the visit? Checking up on Ximena?"

"That's one thing, yes."

A sly smile came over her. "Oooh. I like the sound of that. Mind if I ask the other thing on your mind?" She lifted an eyebrow. Concho wanted to rip the bandage off and tell her was headed north for a day or two and she'd have to watch Ximena for that time, but he could tell she was thinking the same thing he was and he didn't want to break the spell.

"Let me do the checking up first."

Maria walked past him and out into the mall. "Last I saw, she was at the food court. I gave her a few bucks and Randy over at the Burger Barn gave her free drinks all day. She's probably caffeinated up to her eyeballs by now."

Maria pointed to where Ximena sat at a small table overlooking the children's playground, a small area decorated with oversized plastic sculptures of fast food. A young boy was climbing over a giant cheeseburger and his sister was sliding down a milkshake cup on its side.

"Satisfied?"

"Never doubted you for a second."

"Seriously though, I gave a heads-up to pretty much everyone to keep an eye on her. Eduardo in the security office knows not to let her leave the property. She's in good hands."

He took Maria's hand in his. "I know she is. These are *very* good hands."

"Hmm, maybe you want to see what those hands can do? Come back to my office and find out."

She started to lead him back to where she could lock the door. Concho's conscience caught up with him.

"Maria, first I have to tell you something."

"What is it?"

"I need to go check something out for a day or two. And I'm helping out with the Marshal's office on a thing. I'll need you to keep an eye on Ximena for a little while longer."

He waited for the explosion, the yelling, the fiery look in her eyes. Instead he got a defeated sigh.

"Trying to find out more about this Black Wolf guy?"

"Yeah."

"For how long?"

"Should only be a day or two, tops."

She sighed again. "In that case, if I'm not going to see you and since we got interrupted last night, you're gonna have to give me three days worth to tide me over."

With a smile, she pulled him into her office and locked the door behind them. Before Concho could undo his gun belt and set it down on the chair, Maria's skirt was above her hips and her red panties were down at her ankles and she stepped out of them and moved up onto her desk, shoving aside some papers. He moved toward her and they kissed while he undid his belt with one hand and she helped push down his jeans.

"You really gonna miss me?" he asked.

"That depends on the next ten minutes. You better give me something to miss."

Maria pulled him to her. She was ready for him, no preamble at all. They didn't speak, only panted loud breaths in each other's ear. After only a short time, the walkie-talkie on top of the nearby filing cabinet crackled to life.

Eduardo, the security man on duty, came over the line.

"Hey, boss lady, got a code three."

Concho slowed, figuring their time was up. Maria held him close to her. "No," she said. "Don't stop."

She leaned to the side, awkwardly twisting her body and making it difficult for Concho to continue. The acrobatics only seemed to heighten her pleasure. She managed to get the walkie-talkie down from the cabinet. She keyed the side button and breathlessly said, "Deal with it."

Eduardo came back, "Okay, but you said to let you know next time."

"Shoplifting?" Concho asked.

Maria nodded. "Damn it."

"It's a kid," Eduardo said.

"Damn it," Maria repeated. She keyed the walkie again. "Give me two minutes."

She dropped the walkie on the desk and clasped her hands behind Concho's neck.

"Let's go, Ten-Wolves."

Concho sped up, the pressure on.

* * *

A SHORT TIME LATER, STILL FLUSHED AND A LITTLE OUT OF breath, Maria fast-walked to meet Eduardo outside Angelica's Accessories, a jewelry and beauty supply store. Concho walked a few paces behind her, letting her take the lead in her domain. Eduardo pointed to the shoplifter inside.

"Teen girl, dark hair. She's got at least three items in her purse already."

Maria squinted through the window. "I don't recognize her. Not one of our regulars."

"Want me to take her down?"

"Don't, like, tackle her or anything, but yeah. Go pick her up."

"How long has she been in there?" Concho asked.

Eduardo turned to him, gave a quick glance down at his double Colts, but Concho had a moment of panic that he hadn't zipped his fly.

"Don't know, 'Bout fifteen minutes maybe."

Concho turned and looked around the mall for a moment. "Teen girls usually take a bunch of stuff at once?"

All three looked back at the girl as she slipped another bracelet into her purse.

"I guess not. Maybe. Sometimes," Eduardo said.

"What are you getting at?" Maria asked.

"Just wonder if she's working with someone."

Concho glanced around again.

Maria considered it. She tapped Eduardo on the shoulder and stepped back. He followed until all three of them were out of sight should the girl look out the window.

"Leave her alone and when she comes out, follow her," Maria said.

Eduardo looked dubious, but he nodded.

A moment later, the girl stepped out of the store. She didn't look back. She walked with purpose to her right, clutching her handbag tightly to her side. Concho split off from Maria and Eduardo and followed from the other side of the walkway.

They had to hustle to keep up. She turned and went into the food court. Concho spotted Ximena sitting with an extra-large soft drink cup in front of her and still watching the kid's play area. He figured the free drinks were a way of Randy flirting with her.

The young shoplifter sat down at a table where a young man, early twenties, black T-shirt with a gold chain hanging around his neck, bright white brand new pair of basketball shoes that Concho knew were probably hundreds of dollars. He wore his close-cropped hair in tiny spikes and his gold watch looked as wide as a dinner plate.

The girl took the items from her purse and passed them to him. He looked unimpressed even as she smiled, waiting for his approval.

Concho caught Maria's eye from across the room. She smiled at him and he lifted his shoulders and tried to look humble. He mouthed *Lucky guess*.

Maria tapped Eduardo on the shoulder and pointed him in their direction. Eduardo seemed reluctant to go, but Maria gave him one of her firm looks that Concho knew were impossible to disobey. He sheepishly marched toward the table.

Concho watched as Eduardo approached. This was his jurisdiction so Concho held back, here if the security guard needed him, but letting the young man have his bust.

Ximena turned away from the kids briefly, sipping on her drink. She spotted Concho standing nearby and smiled. She waved. Concho waved back but kept his attention on the bust going down across the food court.

The spiky-haired young man bolted out of his seat like he

was on springs. He left the young girl behind as he put one foot on a chair and launched himself across the food court.

Concho tensed and instinctively put a hand on the Colt hanging off his right side. With people around and a children's play area straight ahead, he did not draw.

Eduardo was armed with a taser and he fumbled it from his holster.

"Stop. Freeze!" he shouted.

The young man did not.

Maria stepped up and put a hand on the young girl's shoulder, pinning her down in her seat. The girl seemed in shock at being left behind so quickly.

Concho knew Eduardo was too far away for a taser shot, and the guard stood with feet firmly planted as he called out again for the man to stop. He was headed Concho's way.

Ximena saw Concho's reaction and followed his eyes. By now, a woman had screamed as her tray of fast food had been knocked to the ground while the spiky-haired young man flashed by her.

The man leaped the low boundary wall of the kid's area and vaulted over the oversized plastic cheeseburger. A small boy ducked aside as the man set eyes on the exit doors.

Concho stood firm with his feet shoulder width apart, wishing like hell he didn't have to draw his weapon. He had places to be. If he became the arresting officer on scene it would mean paperwork, delays, explanations to Shaw why he was here at the mall in the first place. But he couldn't simply let this man get away.

With his index finger he undid the snap on his holster and committed himself.

As the young man was in the air coming down from his leap off the cheeseburger. Ximena flung her extra-large drink cup out in front of her. She held tight to the cup and the lid popped off and twenty-four ounces of high-fructose and caffeine splashed on the floor in front of the man. He landed and his hundred dollar shoes went out from under him. With a painful-sounding thud, he landed on his back.

Concho tensed the muscles in his arm and stopped his draw before the Colt cleared the holster. He ran forward and stood over the young man gasping for breath, the wind knocked out of him.

Concho looked over at Ximena who gave him a slightly apologetic look. He smiled at her and she smiled back.

Eduardo crossed the play area, taser still drawn, and stood over the man.

"Freeze!" he said.

The spiky-haired young man writhed on the ground like an insect with his wings pulled off.

Concho looked at Eduardo. "I think you got it from here."

He looked across the food court and found Maria's eyes. He blew her a kiss and walked to the exit.

CHAPTER THIRTEEN

DESPITE THE DELAY IN GETTING ON THE ROAD, CONCHO MADE good time headed north. He arrived at the Marshall office at five forty-five, just in time to catch his contact, Marshall Anthony Toomey.

"Concho Ten-Wolves? Is that right?" Toomey said.

"Yes."

"Well, that sounds like exactly the man we need." Toomey was tall, sandy blond, a swimmer judging from his broad shoulders. He spoke with an East Texas drawl. "I gotta tell you, though," he said. "And I need to speak delicately here given the way of the world these days…but you don't look much like a Native American."

"I know that, Marshall. My father was African American. But I assure you, I am a member of the Kickapoo tribe."

"Well, as long as you can talk the talk and get us close to our man without spooking him, that's all I need from you."

"I'll do my best."

Toomey glanced down at Concho's twin guns. "They sent you well-armed anyway."

"I find it's better to have them and not need them than not to have them at all."

Toomey nodded in agreement at that, then started to pack up his things for the end of the day. "They got you set up at a motel?"

"Yeah, I found a place that's pretty cheap and hopefully pretty clean too."

"One usually doesn't come with the other."

"Sad but true."

"Well, let's say we'll meet here tomorrow at nine a.m. and go over the rollout plan. We should have it wrapped up and get you on your way by noon if all goes well."

"Do they usually go well?"

Toomey pulled on a jacket. He smoothed it out over the bulge of the gun on his belt. "You mean does it usually go well when someone skips bail or runs from the cops and we have to go bring him back into custody? Guys with warrants and long records and more guns than a platoon of Marines? Does that transaction sound like it would go well to you?"

"Not a hundred percent of the time, no."

"Fingers crossed tomorrow is in the good percentage." he stuck out a hand to shake. Concho took it and they both gripped hard. "Thanks for your help, Ranger."

"My pleasure, Marshall."

CHAPTER FOURTEEN

CONCHO'S LONG LEGS WERE BENT AT A PAINFUL ANGLE IN THE back seat of the SUV. Marshal Toomey rode shotgun while a man Concho had met when he got in the car, Marshal Don Vicksburg, drove. Don hadn't said a word since Concho shook his hand and he'd said "Morning" in a flat, unwelcoming tone. They both wore the trademark blue windbreakers with US Marshal on the back in bold letters. Behind them rode two more SUVs filled with armed marshals.

Toomey ran down the case as they headed out of town and into the flat, sandy scrub.

"So, you'll see when we get there that this place is a bit of a compound. It's all Native Americans, but not a Reservation, just a little community-type thing that sprung up. They put it together themselves over the years. Started as just one apartment complex, but then when the strip mall down the road died out and the gas station shut down, nobody was left but them. Started moving in trailer homes and RVs and vans. Like a shanty town, a little bit."

"So they're self-segregating?"

"Yeah, I guess you'd call it that."

"I get it."

Don pointed off to the west where a small rise of low buildings and vehicles grouped along the horizon.

"So this guy, William Bearclaw, he's a slippery so-and-so. Plan is that you go in and try to find out which unit he's in. Say you're a cousin from down south. He's related to a guy named Petey White Horse. Petey's been in lock up for the past twelve and a half years so it's doubtful anyone around will know what he looks like. All I need is for you to get someone there to point you in his direction. once you know, you call us and we'll handle the rest."

Concho checked his watch. If it was as easy as he said, he could get this wrapped up and make it out to the prison just after lunchtime.

"No wire or anything?" Concho asked.

"Nah." Toomey waved the idea away as too involved. "Just shoot me a text, maybe a photo of the place where he's at. We'll storm the gates, so to speak."

Toomey turned in his seat to look at Concho. "I think you'd better leave the pea shooters behind." He gestured to the gun belt around Concho's waist. "Might make some of 'em nervous."

Concho nodded his agreement and began to unbuckle. "This unusual for it to take this many tries at a guy?"

"Nah, not too. If they're on the run, they gotta be somewhat good at it. It's just a matter of time, though. Someone will rat them out. Somebody will get sloppy. We'll be there."

He and Don bumped knuckles together and laughed.

"Seems like you enjoy your job, Marshal."

"I like catching bad guys," Toomey said. "This guy has a warrant and that means he's bad. Wanted for statutory rape on a sixteen-year-old when he was twenty-two. Said they were in love. Then he took her across state lines and robbed a liquor store with her next to him, making her an accessory. Once they picked them both up, he went and ditched her. Left her high and dry, which honestly, bothers me more than the other stuff. Take a girl that young and get her to think she's in love and all that, then you pull a runner when the chips are down? No, man. That's no way to behave. Rob a liquor store and you might be a piece of crap or you might be down on your luck and having a bad day. But run out on a girl who is putting all her trust in you and left everything behind because you sweet-talked her into it—and talked his way into her pants? No way, man. No friggin' way."

The SUV turned off the main road and headed toward the compound.

"Plus," Toomey said. "He's slipped us twice already. That don't sit all that well with me or the Marshall service."

"I'm getting that impression," Concho said.

Don pulled up a few hundred yards from the compound. Concho knew he'd have to walk the rest of the way so as not to spook the residents with a long line of government vehicles.

"Good luck, Ten-Wolves. Go get him."

Concho got out and felt naked without his guns. He started walking down the dusty road toward a large apartment complex.

It seemed to happen quite a lot that buildings in this part of the world were all the same color as the sand. Concho didn't know if they started out painted that way, or if they were all just sun-bleached and faded until everything was the shade of dry brush.

The apartment building had seen better days. Beyond it was a short strip of shops, mostly boarded up and closed down. On either side of the only paved road were trailer homes, double-wides and RVs up on blocks.

Without any better place to start, Concho knocked on the door to apartment number one. After a minute a woman answered, but kept the chain on the door in place. She had a deeply lined face of tan skin and long, straight black hair. She didn't say a word.

"Excuse me, ma'am. My name is Petey White Horse. I'm looking for my cousin, William? William Bearclaw?"

The face just stared at him, impassive.

"Do you know him?"

The door closed. Concho started to think he might not make it out to the prison today. The curtain in the window pulled back a few inches and he could see the same face peering out, checking if he was still there. Concho stepped over to the window and spoke loud through the glass.

"He's my cousin," he said again. "William Bearclaw? Do you know where he lives?"

The face was unmoved but kept up her intense stare. Concho decided to try something.

He asked for William again, only this time in the Kickapoo language. Unimpressed, she did not answer. He tried again in Sauk, another dialect he knew. When that didn't work, he switched to Fox. He brought out all the ammunition he had to prove to her he was Native and could be trusted.

When nothing seemed to work, as a last-ditch, Concho cupped his hands around his mouth and used Kickapoo whistle speech, a form of communication only a real Native would know. He begged her to trust him.

The curtain slid back in place and she was gone.

Concho turned to apartment door number two and debated just starting in on a Native tongue first.

The door to number one opened again, this time without the chain.

A younger woman was there now. Thinner, fewer wrinkles on her face, same dark hair, and intense eyes.

"You looking for William?"

Concho smiled. "Yes, ma'am. I'm his cousin. Been a long while since I seen him."

She looked him up and down, which took a while due to his size. "Mom says you speak with many tongues, and you also wear many skins."

"My parents were mixed."

She nodded at this, accepting the explanation. She stepped out onto the welcome mat which had faded and any message written there had long since disappeared. She pointed down the road. "Third trailer down. Has a blue door. Satellite dish on top."

Concho followed where her finger pointed. "Third one?"

She nodded. He thanked her in his native Kickapoo tongue and stepped into the street toward the line of trailer homes.

Concho walked the empty street, a light wind whistling past his ears. He studied the trailers on the other side of the street. Mostly rusted-out models probably bought at auction for pennies. He wondered if any of them even had working toilets. He counted three and saw the blue door. He took out his cell phone and snapped a photo, then texted it to Toomey with the words *MAIN STREET.*

Concho pocketed his phone and crossed into the shade of a boarded-up sporting goods shop and waiting for the marshals to descend.

He didn't have to wait long. A line of four SUVs barreled down the main drag, kicking dust behind them. No sirens, just V-8 engines. Concho turned his attention to the trailer and he saw the whole unit rock on its soft springs. A small hatch at the top opened and a body crawled out. From the file photo, it looked like William Bearclaw. He looked left, then right. The SUVs ground to a halt in a cloud of dry Texas dust.

William Bearclaw took a running start and leaped from the roof of his trailer to the roof of the one next to his.

Concho watched him leap and was impressed at the man's lithe ability. Marshals began pouring from the SUVs and moved to surround the trailer with the blue door. In the dust cloud, none of them had seen William Bearclaw escape.

"Uh-oh," Concho said to himself.

Toomey led the charge, gun drawn and pointed down he banged a fist on the blue door and shouted, "US Marshals. Open up!"

William Bearclaw was three trailers down by then, using them like stepping stones across a muddy river. Concho started to move, mirroring William Bearclaw's movements to the east and keeping him in sight. With all the shouting of multiple marshals, if he'd called out to them it would have been lost to the wind.

William Bearclaw made one final leap, this one a few feet farther than the others. He barely landed on the roof of the last trailer in line and it looked like he scraped up his leg pretty badly on the fall. Concho was even with him from the opposite side of the street. He stood in front of the first open store he'd come to. A mini-mart and liquor store. The owner stood in the doorway watching the action but was so still Concho thought he was one of those old-time wooden Indians put there as a joke. When the man finally moved, Concho flinched.

"Bearclaw again, huh?" the old man said. His face was lined with deep grooves from a lifetime in the sun. He looked so much like darkly stained wood that Concho didn't feel bad about guessing he was a statue at first. The old man bit off a hunk from a solid square of chewing tobacco.

Concho watched as William Bearclaw dropped off the far end of the trailer and disappeared behind it. He gave a quick glance down the street to the commotion surrounding the trailer with the blue door and saw that nobody was looking this way.

"Damn it," he cursed to himself, knowing this was up to him now.

CHAPTER FIFTEEN

CONCHO CROSSED THE STREET IN A RUN. WHEN HE REACHED the edge of the pavement, he heard an engine start up. Not a big V-8 like the Marshall's SUVs, but a smaller one. Like the flash of a jackrabbit rushing past, Concho saw a 4-wheel ATV come out from behind the last trailer, William Bearclaw in the seat.

Concho changed his trajectory and picked up his pace as he aimed for the path in front of the ATV. William Bearclaw, no helmet on, looked up to see the tall man in front of him and he veered right.

Concho stopped and instinctively reached for his Colt but found only an empty belt. He silently cursed Toomey for making him leave the guns behind. He stayed still as the ATV passed by close enough to cover him in grit from the tires kicking up dust and gravel.

The ATV's escape route had been blocked and William Bearclaw steered the 4-wheeler in between the mini-mart and a closed-up beauty shop. The narrow alley wouldn't have fit a normal-sized car, but the ATV slid in between the two buildings like it was made for the gap.

Concho kept his legs pumping and followed him into the alleyway.

William Bearclaw reached the end and came up to a stack of rotting two-by-fours and a pile of old cinderblocks. The gap between them and freedom was too small even for the ATV. He turned in his seat to see the tall man running after him like someone in a *Terminator* movie.

William quickly moved the ATV into a three-point turn that became more of a five-point turn.

Concho slowed, knowing William was boxed in.

"Marshals are here to take you in, William." He panted for breath, the words taking all the air left in his lungs.

"I know that," William said. "They can go to hell."

He got the ATV around and gunned the little two-stroke engine. The buzz-saw grind of the motor echoed off the walls on either side of Concho as the 4-wheeler bore down on him. There wasn't enough room to safely pass by and William Bearclaw showed no signs of stopping.

Concho took three long strides forward, closing the gap between him and the ATV, then angled left and put a foot on the stucco wall of the old beauty shop, using it to push off and lift him off the ground.

William Bearclaw came by fast, but Concho was flying over him. With his right leg, he kicked out and caught William on the side of his exposed head with the heel of his boot. Bearclaw flopped off the ATV and landed on the ground of the alley. The ATV kept going but slowed as his hand came off the throttle.

Concho landed and rolled, his feet not quite under him for a solid exit from the acrobatic move. He felt skin tear on his shoulder and the palms of his hands. From flat on the ground, he looked up to see William Bearclaw push himself up to his feet and chase after the ATV.

Concho got his own legs under him and started to run.

William vaulted into the seat of the ATV like a cowboy in a movie mounting his horse. Concho's hand swiped by the collar of William's shirt close enough to touch the fabric, but he'd squeezed the throttle on the 4-wheeler and kicked a cloud of dirt in Concho's face as he sped off.

Concho shook his head in frustration and picked up the chase again.

William Bearclaw turned onto the main street. By then, the marshals had realized he wasn't in the trailer with the blue door so Toomey and his comrades were all looking in different directions to see where he could have possibly gone to when the ATV spilled around the corner, then a second later, Concho followed on foot.

Concho could see Toomey directing his team back to the SUVs to get ready to give chase. William Bearclaw saw it too. He knew his tiny ATV didn't stand a chance against four SUVs. They approached the corner of the apartment building and William veered right. The gate that once gave some semblance of security to the complex had rusted away years ago and a lengthy gap gave William plenty of space to pilot the SUV through, but he had to move slowly. Concho didn't know how much more he had left in him at a dead sprint, but when he saw William Bearclaw carefully picking his way over rusty fence beams and dead bushes from the former landscaping, he kept his legs pumping.

All four SUVs came to life at the same time and the air was again filled with swirling dust.

Concho followed William as he drove the ATV into the center of the apartment complex. It was a two-story horseshoe shape around a center courtyard and an old swimming pool. A single palm tree hung on for dear life as the only living vestige of the former landscaping.

Concho vaulted himself over the dead bushes and the rusted fence and was inside the complex. He spotted a person on the second floor standing in their doorway watching while smoking a cigarette.

Ahead of him, William Bearclaw gunned the tiny engine and the rear wheels fishtailed out a little. William tried to wrestle the machine back in line, but it wouldn't cooperate. Concho watched as William dipped over the edge of the pool.

There was no splash. No cascade of water. The pool was dry. Probably had been for years. Concho heard a long rev of the engine amplified by the concave sound chamber of the dry swimming pool, then the ATV rode the slow curve of the bowl and launched into the air. William was not on board.

The ATV shot straight up fifteen feet, then came crashing down on top of what used to be a small shed for pool supplies. The engine finally died.

Concho leaned forward over the edge of the pool. At the bottom, splayed out over the drain, was William Bearclaw, moaning and clutching his leg which was bent at an angle no leg should ever bend.

A rush of footsteps like migrating elks came up behind Concho and he turned to see Toomey leading a small cadre of his team, guns drawn and all sweating in their US Marshall's windbreakers.

Toomey peered over the edge of the pool, then looked at Concho.

"So," Concho said. "Can I get a ride back to my hotel? I want to make it out to the prison, still."

CHAPTER SIXTEEN

CONCHO DIDN'T MAKE IT BACK TO HIS HOTEL UNTIL AFTER TWO o'clock, the little detour to apprehend William Bearclaw had eaten up most of his day and when he called the prison to set a meeting with the warden, he was told Warden Scalise wouldn't be seeing anyone for the rest of the day. Performance reviews were due. So Concho set a meeting at ten a.m. the next morning and, after a long shower, set out to get something to eat.

All that running and chasing had given him a powerful appetite. He drove out near the prison, knowing that a town like this sitting in the middle of a whole lot of nothing would cling to a job-creator like a prison as a lifeline. Whole communities build up around most prisons, even the small ones like the William "Bigfoot" Wallace Unit where The Black Wolf was kept.

With only a short window to gather information, he figured he might as well turn a late lunch into a little fact-finding mission as well.

He found a diner with a sign on a twenty-foot pole out front that simply said EAT. Concho parked his truck and went inside.

Twangy country music played over old, blown-out speakers. Old-time songs, not the modern pop country. The place smelled like fry grease and a time not too long ago when most people smoked inside a restaurant. There were signs on the inside as plain-spoken as the sign out front. HOT COFFEE. APPLE PIE. CASH ONLY. Not one for a whole lot of words, these diner folks.

Concho stood inside the door and took it all in. There was a long counter and a row of booths along the windows. One booth was occupied by an older couple, there for a late lunch like Concho or maybe an early dinner. He wasn't sure. One man occupied the last stool at the counter and he looked like he came with the fixtures.

There were two waitresses behind the counter, one putting away forks and spoons into a caddy and the other filing her nails. The one with the nail file looked up and then kept right on filing. The other waitress said, "Anywhere you like."

Concho sat at the counter. The waitress finished putting away the silverware and brought him a laminated menu.

"Coffee?" she asked.

"No, thanks."

Concho turned over the one-page menu and surveyed the options, of which there were few. He read the waitress's name tag, JUNE, before she returned the coffee pot to the burner and let it scald. She came back with a small notepad and pencil in her hands.

"Would you say the burger is a safe bet?" Concho asked.

"It won't kill ya," she answered.

He set down the menu. "Good enough for me."

June scribbled on her pad and said, "Fries," more as a statement than a question.

"Sure. No pickles."

"Right."

She tore off the top sheet on her pad and went to put it on the spinning carousel hanging in the pass-through to the kitchen.

"Order up!" She rang a small bell. She brought water in a sweating plastic pitcher to Concho's seat at the counter and poured him a glass.

"You don't want nothin' else to drink?"

"No, ma'am. This is fine." He took a sip and it tasted like rust and minerals, so he set the glass down.

"You visiting someone?" June asked, with a nod in the direction of the prison.

"Tomorrow," he said.

"Only strangers we get around here are visiting someone. You don't look like no lawyer. You got kin in there?"

"No. Just asking a few questions of the warden."

She lifted an eyebrow at him, curious now. "What for?"

"Work," he said. He unbuttoned the breast pocket of his western shirt and drew out his badge. He held it out for June so she could read that he was a ranger.

"Always some kind of cop or lawyer or fed coming through here. You already got 'em locked up, what more do you need to know?"

Concho nodded to the girl filing her nails. "I'd like to know why you're doing all the work around here."

June followed his eyes and when she saw the other girl, June scoffed. "Jean-Marie? Hell, her husband owns the place. She don't never do no work."

"She's dressed like a waitress," he said, referring to the pink top, name tag, and pink hair clip they both wore.

"Trust me, you don't want her anywhere near your food. Unless you like eating your lunch off your lap."

"I sure don't."

June set the pitcher down and then turned back to Concho. "Wait, you're trying to distract me. You didn't answer my question."

"What question?"

"What business you have up at the prison."

"That, ma'am, I'm afraid is official business."

She folded her arms across her chest. "Well, damn. I

thought I was gonna have an interesting conversation for once around here. Get a real live Texas Ranger who looks like... well, like *you*, and I figure I'm in for at least a few war stories."

"I'd think living so close to the prison you get all kinds of stories."

"Nah." She waved the idea away. "Those big ol' walls don't only keep the people in, they keep the gossip in as well. You know much interesting stuff is happening right now just beyond that razor wire?"

"I shudder to think."

"Them boys think they got the boring side of things, being locked up all day like that. I'm here to tell you, I know for a fact life inside that prison is ten times as excitin' as what goes on out here."

The man at the end of the corner called out, "June. Coffee."

She rolled her eyes so Concho could see and snatched up the coffee pot on her way to the end of the counter. She refilled the man's cup without a word and he offered no thank you when she left him. She set the pot back on the burner and returned to Concho. Jean-Marie kept on filing. Concho figured she'd be down to the quick before much longer.

"So where was I?" June asked.

"You said you know about what goes on behind the walls."

"Huh." She folded her arms again. "Too well. My ex, he used to be a guard up there. Well, still is. He just ain't my husband anymore."

Concho set his elbows on the counter and leaned on them. "Yeah? He used to tell you stuff?"

"The man couldn't keep his thing in his pants and he couldn't keep a secret. Top two reasons I divorced him. But it's a long list."

Concho set his ranger badge on the counter, let the shield catch the light. "He ever mention someone they call The Black Wolf?"

June lifted her chin and looked down her nose at him. "That who you're up here to see?"

"In a way."

"Trust me, you don't want nothing to do with that man."

"Why is that?"

June leaned forward and set her folded arms on the counter, put her face right up close to Concho so she could speak low.

"That's a bad, bad man."

"So I've heard."

"You ain't heard nothing, I'm telling you. Whatever you think you know is the Reader's Digest version. Roy used to say, that's my ex-husband, Roy, he used to say that man was the devil on earth."

June gave a worried look over her shoulder to Jean-Marie.

The bell rang. "Order up."

Concho put a hand on her arm before she could.stand up straight. "Would you be willing to talk to me a little after your shift?"

June glanced right, then left. "Eight o'clock."

She turned and got the plate from the pass-through and then set the saddest-looking hamburger Concho had ever seen before him.

"You said it won't kill me, right?"

"Said it won't kill you. Didn't say it won't make you sick."

CHAPTER SEVENTEEN

THE WILLIAM "BIGFOOT" WALLACE UNIT WAS A SMALL PRISON by Texas standards. It kept the inmate population low so each offender could get the proper attention. In a prison system filled with bad men, these were the worst ones. No minor drug offenders, no traffic violations, no domestic abusers. The six hundred and fifteen men inside the walls of Bigfoot, as it was known inside, had made deals with the devil and they knew this would be the last residence they'd ever see on this earth.

William Wallace was a Texas ranger in the 1800s and his nickname, Bigfoot, was earned due to his size. When an inmate found out they were headed to Bigfoot it was like the sign says, ABANDON HOPE ALL YE WHO ENTER HERE.

The Black Wolf reclined in a chair while another inmate rubbed his feet. He lived a life of contrasts – awful food served behind twenty-foot walls and concertina wire. Men with rifles in parapets watching his daily two hours of outdoor time. A thin mattress on a metal cot with a hard, flat pillow.

And yet, he never did labor, managed to eat chocolate, drink whiskey, shower alone, smoke Cuban cigars and still run operations of the empire he'd built before he was arrested.

He paid off guards, or rather his lieutenants did, he'd had

six other inmates killed in his time behind the walls of Bigfoot Unit. He picked the films for movie night. He lived like a king in bondage.

The cell door stood open and the sounds of the cell block echoed in the concrete and steel bunker of block two, where The Black Wolf had lived for the past nine years. A guard appeared in the open doorway. A short, stout man, his name tag read ELWIN.

The Black Wolf looked up, but the man at his feet never stopped rubbing.

"Ah, Douglas, come in."

Douglas Elwin stayed in the hallway, one hand resting on his nightstick. "What do you need? I only have a minute."

"My message got to you that we needed to talk?"

"I'm here, ain't I?"

"So I see."

The Black Wolf had affected a thick accent gleaned mostly from the movie *Scarface*, so his Mexican accent had transitioned to more of a Cuba-via-Miami.

"I want to know the progress."

Elwin looked annoyed. He glanced down at the man rubbing The Black Wolf's feet. He knew the inmate from block one and figured he was working off some penance for a very minor transgression. If there was no blood involved, it couldn't be very serious. The Black Wolf wanted blood for not returning a "good morning" greeting.

"Don't mind him," The Black Wolf said.

"Things are coming along," Elwin said. "These things take time."

"I know they do. But the clock, she is ticking, and I swore I would not make it ten years in this place."

"Okay, look, I can't just snap my fingers and spring you from a place like this. It takes planning and coordination. I'm working with James Lee and he's got to get his side of things set up. You just have to sit tight."

The Black Wolf gave a weak smile. Elwin didn't like the look.

"If you want to grease some more palms," Elwin said. "Maybe we could speed things up, but I don't think even you have the cash to take care of everyone between here and the border. Plus, everyone involved is also trying to protect their own asses. And you want it done right, don't you?"

"Yes, I do. Of course."

"Because if they catch you once busting out, they make damn sure it can't happen a second time. That means solitary, that means loss of privileges. And I don't see why you're so damn eager to bust out of here anyway." Elwin pointed at the man rubbing his feet, the bottles of liquor lined against the wall. "You got it pretty good."

"Perhaps you want to trade places."

Elwin shifted under the stare.

"Look, I'm doing my best, okay? I'll touch base with James Lee again, see where we're at. Okay?"

"Very well. Tell James Lee I want to talk to him. It's been too long."

"Anything else?"

"Just this." The Black Wolf set his feet on the floor. The man bent in front of him cowered away. He stared up at Douglas Elwin and spoke calmly and slowly. "You would do well to talk to me with more respect. Remember what I pay. And remember that when I am out, it will be that much easier for me to visit your home and find your daughter, Annie, and your wife, Shanise. And think about what it would be like to come home to find your house painted in their blood. To find your wife's tongue cut out and waiting for you on the kitchen counter. Your daughter's eyeballs floating in the toilet. Think about how I could do that tomorrow, but it would rob me of the satisfaction of watching them die myself. So when I ask when the plans will be set in motion, I don't expect more delays. I expect you to stick to your promises. I expect to be out of here before I hit ten years. I expect to never have to see you or this place again. But know that I will *always* know where you are."

Elwin tried to swallow but it was like a rock got caught in his throat. The Black Wolf waved him away and Elwin turned on his heel and practically ran.

The Black Wolf settled back in his chair and lifted his foot back into the palm of the man on his knees. He leaned back and closed his eyes, trying to block out the noise from the cell block.

"He wants me to stay," he said. "The longer I stay, the longer he gets paid. I know how it is. If you own any kind of business, I don't care if it's an ice cream shop, you should expect people to skim a little. Take advantage. It's only natural. But there is a limit."

CHAPTER EIGHTEEN

Concho shifted in his seat, the burger not settling well. He waited outside the diner for June to clock out. At eight on the dot, she came through the glass doors and let out a long exhale. She reached up and took out the band that had been holding her hair up in a bun and it fell down past her shoulders in a tangle.

She looked around the parking lot and Concho flashed his lights to call her over. She got in the passenger side of his truck.

"So where to, ranger man?" she said.

"You tell me. We can just sit here and talk or I'll take you wherever you want."

"Lord, I don't want to hang around here even a second longer than I have to. Let's go out to the coffee place off Durango Street. They have food, too."

"You don't get a free meal when you work a shift?"

"I wouldn't eat Jack's food free, or even if he paid me to."

Concho's stomach rumbled again. "Yeah, I know what you mean."

He started up the truck and followed her directions to a place on the corner of the main drag. A small group of teenagers sat at an outside table getting a caffeine fix to keep going all night if they needed to. Inside it was quieter with jazz on the stereo and low lighting. June ordered a large black coffee and a pastry covered in icing.

"I got this," Concho said, stepping up and removing his wallet.

"Damn right you do," June said, taking her coffee and going to find a seat.

Concho ordered a black tea and put three packets of sugar in it. He joined her in a booth near the back door.

"I'm lucky I ran into you," he said.

"It's a small town. You throw a rock and you hit three people with ties to the prison. So what do you want to know about Bigfoot?"

"Less the place as a whole and more one inmate."

"The Black Wolf?"

Concho nodded. He told her the story of Ximena and what he'd learned so far. He didn't love spilling his case out to a civilian, but he had no reason not to trust her and he needed more information before his meeting with the warden in the morning.

"So does that make sense that he would be moving girls across the border?" he asked her.

"More than you know," she said. "Look, I told you Roy liked to dip his wick outside of our marital bedroom, right? Well, this Black Wolf guy still has juice on the outside and he didn't like the idea of being locked up with only the fellas for all those years. You know what happens to a lot of them guys when they're away from the feminine charms for such a long time? Well, this Black Wolf, he decides he's just gonna get the girls to come to him."

"So they visit him at prison for…conjugal visits?"

"If that means he has sex with them, then yes. Only they don't come by choice."

"Wait, are you saying that Roy…?"

June nodded. "Yup. This Black Wolf paid off guards to look the other way and let the girls in, you know? Some of that payment was they got to have a go with the girls after he was done with them. They'd get passed around like a joint at a Grateful Dead concert. Poor things."

She sipped her coffee and took a bite of pastry thinking of the poor kidnapped girls.

"So, Ximena was on her way to the prison to be offered up to The Black Wolf and whoever else wanted their turn?"

"Basically, yeah."

Concho's stomach roiled and it had nothing to do with the burger from earlier.

"So he pays off guards?"

She nodded again. "Enough to get whatever he wants brought in."

"Does the warden know?"

"I bet he's got to have some notion. I don't know if he's on the take or for how much if he is. All I know is he's not stupid enough to piss off The Black Wolf. Even if he ain't taking a payoff, he won't get in his way because he likes all his fingers and his working kneecaps. Hell, he likes being above ground. Black Wolf has that kind of reach. Money'll do that."

Concho knew that was true. "Thank you, June. This is a big help."

"Saying it all like this makes me feel like a fool I never did nothing to stop it."

"It's hard with men like this. When the threat of violence is real, it becomes very effective."

"And when I was married to Roy, I didn't want nothing to rock the boat, you know? I won't lie, the extra money was all right too. But I swear to you, I didn't know about it until right there at the end. It wasn't like I was living high on the hog off that money for a long time and turned a blind eye to what was happening."

"It's okay, June. You're doing the right thing now."

A sudden panic came over her. "But you'll keep my name out of it, right? He won't know it was me who told you."

"No, of course not. This is just between you and me. I'll

make sure it never gets back to The Black Wolf."

"The one you gotta watch out for is James Lee Morris."

"Who's that?"

"Black Wolf's right-hand man on the outside. Used to be a guard. Up there more than ten years. When The Black Wolf showed up, he decided he liked that payday much more and he could make a whole hell of a lot more if he quit being a guard and went to work for The Black Wolf. He cracks skulls for the Wolf now full-time and he's a mean motor scooter."

"James Lee Morris. I'll keep an eye out."

June fixed him with an unconvinced eye. "You're a big one and you got those pea shooters on your hip, plus you got that swagger most Rangers got whether it's earned or not, but I'm telling you, you best beware."

"I hear you."

She finished off her pastry, charged by the sugar rush. "So what say you take me out for a real drink."

"Still thirsty?"

"I mean a Tennessee whiskey. In place with real music that don't try to put me to sleep."

"I'm afraid I have an early morning. Happy to drop you someplace, though."

She waved him away. "Nah. The Butcher's Apron is only two doors down. They got cheap drinks and a live band. Maybe I can drink away the memory of working at that greasy dive."

"I appreciate your time and the information, June."

"You gonna bust the son-of-a-bitch?"

"I'm not sure what's gonna happen yet. He's already behind bars. I just want to make sure no more girls get taken from down south. He's been pulling them off the Rez. That hits home for me. I aim to stop it."

"Yeah, well, if you see Roy up there, go ahead and shoot first, will ya?"

"I know you're only joking, June."

"Then you don't know much, Ranger."

CHAPTER NINETEEN

JAMES LEE MORRIS HUNG UP THE PHONE. HE HATED THAT SO many of his dealings were with people south of the border. There used to be a time when you could cross at will. Nobody cared. Not these days.

Most of these issues would be handled much easier face to face. Intimidation is a personal game, not easily done over a phone line. If he wanted someone to know he was serious, it was hard to do just with his voice.

He'd chewed out the Mexican men who had scooped up the last girl. Something had gone wrong. He didn't fully know what yet, but the girl hadn't arrived and nobody had heard from Ricky since. There was a small chance, James Lee thought, that Ricky could have taken off with the girl, but that wasn't likely. It couldn't have been like a movie where somehow the kidnapped girl falls in love with her captor and they run away to be together. Ricky wasn't near that charming. No, something went wrong in the supply chain.

He knew the guys down south didn't have much to do with the girls once they came north, but he needed someone to chew out and with the others missing, they had to do.

Every time he got frustrated with his job, he thought of the money. Monthly payments came wire transferred into an account for him. Tens of thousands of dollars. Far more than he'd made working at the prison. And he knows only a drop in the bucket of what The Black Wolf pulled down each month.

Now the boss man wanted out.

They'd been planning the break for months. It was a logistical nightmare and not something James Lee was used to coordinating. He thought he had all the pieces in place, had greased all the right palms. He had people in place at Bigfoot, at the border, the highway patrol. They'd break out the Wolf at midnight and be across into Mexico by sunrise.

Then he had a choice to make. Keep taking the money, even if his duties would be reduced to errand boy once the boss man was outside and down south. Or go to Mexico and join ranks with the cartel down there. James Lee had no intention of leaving the USA. He could still be useful as the man north of the border.

Useful at the same pay rate? That he wasn't so sure.

And he'd seen his share of cleanups that The Black Wolf had performed after any big move. Run someone out of a territory? Kill everyone left behind in that operation. Negotiate a merger with a small player? Kill everyone associated with them and start from scratch.

James Lee knew there was a good chance part of The Black Wolf's re-ascension to power would be cleaning house. So part of what he had planned for the big break was his own vanishing act. He had plenty of money stashed away. He lived simply, and in this dusty corner of West Texas, it was hard to live lavishly. He had enough to head to the islands and start fresh. Not enough to last the rest of his life, but enough to buy a small place in a quiet corner and get by on very little.

If it came to that. First things first—get The Black Wolf spring from the Bigfoot Unit.

There was a knock at the door. James Lee reached for the gun next to the couch. Always nearby. Always loaded.

He stopped off on the way to the front door at the small

desk in the entryway and checked the cameras. Six angles, front and back. He clicked the mouse on the small screen where he could see the front door and a figure standing there and the shot went full screen on the nineteen-inch monitor.

It was the guard Douglas Elwin.

James Lee tucked the piece in his belt behind his back and answered the door.

"You know I don't like unannounced visits."

Elwin winched. "Crap. Sorry, man."

"What is it?"

"He wants to see you. Says it's been too long. I think he's getting antsy about the break-out."

"Did you tell him it's all on track?"

"Yeah. He says he doesn't want to stay past his ten years."

James Lee let out a long exhale. "Okay. I'll try to get up there tomorrow."

"Be sure and tell him I told you right away."

"Yeah, yeah. You'll get full credit, Elwin."

"You know how he gets."

"Yeah," James Lee said. "I know better than anyone."

He slammed the door in Elwin's face.

CHAPTER TWENTY

June had always been a lightweight with her liquor. After two full hours at the Butcher's Apron, she'd had enough to send a college sorority girl on a blackout. The Butcher's Apron was a slice of Ye Olde Merry England in the middle of dry, dusty Texas, with the exception of a country and western-only music policy. Some things were sacred.

It was dark wood, cracked leather on the stools, a dart-board, a hand-carved sign out front and Guinness on tap, though ninety percent of the patrons drank from longneck Budweisers and cans of Lone Star.

June had started with a beer and a whiskey shot on the side. After a second one of those she ditched the beer and downed two more shots of straight whiskey. She'd been quiet and paid for each round as she went so the bartender paid her no mind when he refilled her shot glass and therefore had no idea how blitzed she had become.

When she wobbled off the stool to visit the ladies' room it was the first time she realized it herself. Sitting still, the edges had become blurred and the music a little muted in her ears, but trying to find her balance walking upright gave away how drunk she truly was.

She picked her way slowly across the floor, stopping when she needed to, leaning on the bar rail and an empty stool to stay upright. Everyone ignored her, as too often happens with women her age in a bar. Nobody would give her a second look until last call when the options were slim. Maybe then someone would try to buy her a drink instead of her paying for all of it herself.

She welcomed the time in the restroom to sit and breathe deep and try to sober herself by sheer will. She stayed in the stall a long time and as long as nobody came knocking, she felt fine about it. When she stood again, the spins came back and the world tilted a little.

She knew she was done for the night as far as drinks went, but she needed some time to sit still and even out before she called a cab and headed home.

June slowly made her way back toward her stool at the bar like she was navigating a house of mirrors in an earthquake with one eye closed. She had almost made it to safe ground ready to sit quietly and listen to some music, eat a few salted peanuts and sober up when she saw him.

A switch flipped and all reason went out the window. It's what her ex-husband did to her every damn time.

She stumbled past her stool and went for the booth where Roy sat with a woman who looked like she had put on her makeup in a moving car driving over an unpaved highway. Wide smears of lipstick, dark splotches of eyeshadow and enough rouge on her cheeks to apply for clown college. June was prettier than this woman and she knew it.

"Well, speak of the devil and he shall appear," June said.

She swayed a little as Roy looked up from his date and noticed her. The smile on his face slid off. Roy was no catch, either. Midforties, balding, doughy middle, and hair in his ears. But something about losing her husband still lit a fire in June that she had trouble putting out.

"June," he said and left it at that.

"I was just talking about you," she said.

"You're drunk."

She scoffed but didn't try to deny it. "I'm a grown woman. I can have a damn drink."

"What do you want, June?"

Roy's date looked annoyed.

"Just to tell you that I was talking about you," June said.

"Okay then."

She had hoped this would rile him or annoy him, but she got nothing from him. "Yeah," she said. "Party time is over, Roy."

"June, just call a damn cab and leave us be."

"You didn't even introduce me."

Roy sighed. "June, this is—"

"I don't even give a crap." She eyed the other woman. "She looks like forty miles of bad road."

The other woman was insulted and looked to Roy to defend her.

"There's no call for that kind of talk."

June made a *pssht!* sound, and ended up spitting little droplets onto their table.

"Damn it, June!"

June leaned over and lowered her voice, like she was telling him a secret, but with a smile on her face. "I told him everything, Roy. Every. Single. Thing."

"What in the Sam Hill are you talking about, woman?"

June set one elbow on their table to steady herself. "The ranger. I told him all what y'all been doing up there. At the Bigfoot."

Roy looked confused and concerned. "What ranger?"

"Big man who come to see me. Handsome too. Wore two guns." She pantomimed gun fingers and drew both from her hips and fired imaginary shots with a few "pew, pew" sound effects thrown in.

"Make sense, woman. What ranger? And what did you tell him?"

She saw she had gotten to him now. She smiled smugly. "I

told him all about you and the—" She dropped to a whisper. "Black wolf." She topped it off with a wink.

Roy's face dropped. He reached out and grabbed her wrist, holding her tight in place.

"June, I need you to tell me exactly what you said and who you said it to."

She tried to pull away, but he held firm.

The other woman had lost patience with this. "Roy, make her go away."

"Not now, Ailene. Just shut up and drink your beer."

Ailene looked wounded, but she took a pull on her Budweiser.

"Come on, June. Are you making this up? What'd you say?"

Her smile was gone now. "I told him the truth. About the girls, about all of it. How you're a little lap dog for that man. How you take his drug money and let him sin all over that place where he's supposed to be being punished."

"God dammit, June. If you did…"

She let loose one big, barking, "Ha!" She ripped her arm away, leaving scratch marks on her wrist from his nails. "You bet I did. Like I said, Roy. Party time is over."

He stood and took hold of her elbow. "I'm taking you home and you're gonna tell me everything you said and you're gonna tell me this ranger's name."

"Let go of me."

Ailene pouted in the booth. "Roy, what about me?"

"Take a cab."

He threw down a twenty dollar bill on the table and rushed June out of the bar, her feet struggling to catch up with his pace.

CHAPTER TWENTY-ONE

THE WILLIAM "BIGFOOT" WALLACE PRISON WAS A BLAND, TAN rectangle of high walls topped with barbed wire and little else to distinguish it and the men inside. It stood low, only two stories tall, but spread out wide covering the whole block. Nothing about it looked dangerous and as Concho drove through the gates, he thought about how often that is the case with the most dangerous things in the world.

The warden's offices were set apart from the cell blocks, but as Concho got out of his truck he could hear the inmates in the courtyard on exercise break. He spotted a parapet with an armed guard on patrol looking down on the action with a rifle casually slung in his arms like a sleeping baby.

A white-haired secretary sat behind a large desk arranging some papers into a file folder. He wondered if she ever saw the men imprisoned here or if she lived in blissful denial, like most of the people surrounding Bigfoot. Unaware of the evil inside these walls.

"May I help you?" she asked.

"Concho Ten-Wolves here to see Warden Scalise."

She smiled slightly. "I'll let him know you're here."

The outer office was as bland as the rest of the building. Beige carpet, off-white walls, a single rubber tree plant in the corner and framed black-and-white photos on the walls of past wardens and notable figures like the State Director of Prisons and the Governor.

"You may go right in, Mr.…Ten-Wolves was it?"

"Yes, ma'am. Thank you."

He passed by her desk and through the doors to the warden's office. Concho had taken his badge out of his pocket and wore it on the front of his shirt. His nod to formality. He was constantly being pressured to wear his ranger hat more often and dress more immediately recognizable as a Texas Ranger, but he stayed steadfast in his own way of doing the job.

Warden Frank Scalise stood from behind his desk. He was a short man, round in the middle and dark hair slicked back off his forehead. To look at him, you'd expect he was about to open his mouth and start speaking like an extra in *The Godfather*, but when he did, Concho heard a deep Texas drawl dripping with BBQ sauce.

"Howdy, Ranger. Concho Ten-Wolves, do I have that right?"

"Yes, Warden, you do."

Concho took the handshake on offer and Scalise pumped his hand like he expected it to give up some Texas oil.

"That's some moniker your daddy gave you."

Concho didn't have time to explain all that went into his father and their relationship. He simply smiled and nodded.

"It is, yes, sir."

"Well, sit, sit. Can I get you anything to drink? Coke? Iced Tea? Something stronger?"

"No, thank you, Warden."

Scalise settled back into his tall leather chair. He crossed one leg over the knee of the other showing off his oxblood red cowboy boots with silver and turquoise embellishments.

"So, what can I do you for today? Always happy to help out the Rangers any way I can."

Concho sat across from him in a plush leather armchair. The air inside the office was a cool sixty-nine degrees and once Concho settled in he could hear the faint sound of country music playing on speakers somewhere, but they were turned so low he wasn't sure if the warden had forgotten and left it on by mistake or if he had the hearing of a bat.

"I'm here about one of your inmates. Goes by the nickname The Black Wolf."

"Ah," said the warden. "Fulgencio Labante. Yes, I know him well. Been our guest coming on ten years now. With plans to stay on many, many more."

"I'm curious, Warden, if you know whether he might be still running some facets of his operation from inside these walls."

"Running things?"

"It's not unheard of. Cartel leaders go inside, maintain contacts, keep pulling strings from behind bars."

Warden Scalise furrowed his brows at Concho. "This about anything in particular or you just curious?"

Concho ran down the story of Ximena and the supply line of girls coming up to Bigfoot.

"That's one aspect of his business I can link to him. I'm sure there is more."

"And where are you getting this? From the girl?"

"I have a reliable source to corroborate my findings so far."

"Who? What source?"

Concho spread his hands. "I'm afraid I can't reveal my source just at the moment."

Scalise's forehead was now knitting into a permanent scowl. "So you come up here with some cock and bull story that you can't tell me who sold it to you, make it seem like I'm letting the inmates run the show up here? Is that it?"

"No, Warden. Not at all."

"You think I'm on this man's payroll?"

"Not you, sir. But some of the guards, yes. Again, it wouldn't be the first time something like this has happened."

"You ever worked in a prison, Mr. Two-Wolves?"

"It's Ten-Wolves."

"However many goddamn wolves you want. You ever worked in a prison?"

Concho shook his head and tried to look contrite. "No, sir."

"Then allow me to enlighten you about the reality of it. No matter what we do, there's gonna be hierarchies on the block. Some men are born leaders, some are followers. We let that natural process play out so as to avoid conflict with the prisoners. The Black Wolf, and no, nobody around here calls him Fulgencio, he's an alpha dog, see? But rather than me try to keep my foot on his neck, I let him have some freedoms within these walls and he keeps the other dogs in line. Makes all our lives easier. But let me tell you, ranger man, it all stays inside the walls. And there is no doubt about who's in charge. Me." He jammed a thumb into his chest so hard Concho figured it must have hurt, but he made his point.

"Now you come up here and accuse me of letting him run some sort of brothel under my roof? That he might still be running a drug cartel from his tiny cell in cellblock two? You got no evidence but a Mexican girl and some unknown informant. And you come in here to tell me I gotta get my house in order? Who the hell do you think you are?"

"I'm just following the leads where they go."

Scalise ran a hand across his scalp, pushing back his hair even further on his head. "Well, you're just a walking contradiction, ain't you, son? You got an Indian name, you look black as Richard Pryor, you say you're a ranger and yet you come in here and insult a man operating a different branch of the same law enforcement service you claim to serve. So let me ask you again—who the hell do you think you are?"

Concho settled him with a look for a long time. He was trying to read his face, looking for fear, for a lie, for a confession.

"Who I am is someone who trusts what I see and what I hear from the right people. There's something going on up here and it has to do with that inmate. You told me yourself, you give him a long leash. Don't you think it's possible he's taking advantage of that?"

"Don't you think it's possible you've been fed a whole truckload of bull crap and you're buying it like little corn husk dolls y'all sell at those casinos you run?"

Concho held his temper in check. This meeting hadn't gone the way he planned, though he wasn't entirely sure what he expected. It would be nearly impossible for the activities he suspected to go on with the Warden knowing some of it. He might not be implicit in all of it, but if he was as innocent as he claimed, then it meant the man was also an idiot.

"So I take it you are telling me none of these allegations have any truth to them as you know it."

"Not a goddamn one of them. And I'd thank you not to go and repeat them to your superiors. Unfounded rumor and innuendo, that's all it is. Sour grapes from some ex-employee? Some ulterior motive of yours I don't know about yet? All I know is I gave you a valuable part of my morning and all you did was come in here and tell me I don't know what the hell is going on in my own cell blocks."

"All I wanted to do was to report to you the information I've found out."

"Well, it's all a bunch of lies. So put that in your peace pipe and smoke it."

Scalise folded his arms across his chest. Concho took that as a sign the meeting was over. He resisted the urge to reach over the desk and choke the man with his own string tie.

"Sorry I wasted your time, Warden."

Concho stood. The warden didn't. With Scalise in his chair,

Concho loomed over him, his two Colts at eye level with the warden.

"Just so you know," Concho said. "I'm still going to investigate. And wherever the truth leads, even if it's right back to this office, I'm going to follow it."

He turned and walked out.

CHAPTER TWENTY-TWO

He nearly bumped into Roy as he made his way out of the office, though Concho didn't know who he was. He was just another guard in a beige uniform, not June's ex-husband who was on the payroll from The Black Wolf.

Roy noticed him, though. The ranger badge clipped to his shirt pocket gave Concho away even more than his height and his twin Colts. Roy kept a watchful eye on him as Concho headed for the exit.

Roy was coming on shift and he made his first stop cell block two, second floor. The Black Wolf was in his cell, door ajar. Nobody with him. He sat in a chair with a cell phone in hand flipping through short videos on social media. A contraband item for inmates, and one The Black Wolf had access to whenever he wanted. Men like Roy looked the other way and took their monthly cash envelopes to let it slide.

"We might have a problem," Roy said.

The Black Wolf slowly set down the phone on his cot. He eyed Roy with a hard stare.

"What kind of problem?"

"I ran into my bitch ex-wife last night and she was skunk-drunk. Said she told some tales to a Texas Ranger. And now I just seen one coming out of the warden's office."

"A ranger? Here?"

"Yep. Tall black guy or an Indian. I couldn't tell which, he was moving fast."

The Black Wolf pursed his lips, thinking. "What do you think she told him?"

"She said she gave away the game on the girls, the whiskey, the whole damn enchilada."

"And you believe her? How drunk was she?"

"Pretty hammered, but why would she make that up? And then why was a ranger here all of a sudden? Don't make sense."

"We are in Texas."

Roy hung his head, hooked his thumbs in his belt. "I dunno, man. I'm worried it's bad."

The Black Wolf stood. Roy instinctively took a small step back away from him.

"Are you here to tell me you're worried," The Black Wolf said, advancing on him. "Or here to tell me what you're gonna do about it?"

"What the hell can I do about it? If the words already come out of her mouth I can't go stuff 'em back in."

The Black Wolf nodded a slow acknowledgment.

Another guard approached, his boots loud along the concrete floor. He stopped in the open cell door next to Roy and said to The Black Wolf, "You got a visitor."

"That'll be James Lee. I'll give him this information. He's good at handling things like this."

The Black Wolf stepped forward and both guards parted to let him through.

* * *

JAMES LEE MORRIS WAITED IN THE VISITING AREA. THERE WERE four open, hexagonal tables with stools bolted to the floor. No barriers and phones to communicate with, just mint-colored paint on the walls and security cameras in each corner of the room.

James Lee puffed on a cigarette while standing beneath a No Smoking sign.

The door opened and a guard led The Black Wolf into the room. Other signs adorned the walls. A No Eating sign was bolted near the door. A larger sign warned All Conversations Subject To Monitoring Except For Meetings With Legal Counsel.

James Lee ground out the cigarette under his boot. The Black Wolf turned to the guard. "Wait outside." The guard turned but The Black Wolf called him back in. "Monitors," he said.

The guard reached up and pulled the coaxial cable from each camera until the room was cut off from view of the rest of the prison. The guard left and the two men were alone. The Black Wolf sat.

"What do you need?" James Lee asked.

"Information."

"Okay, about what?"

"First, no girls."

James Lee stuffed his hands in his front pockets. "There was an issue with the last delivery. Fresh meat is on the way."

"An issue I should know about?"

"No. Nothing major. Just a nosy ranger is all."

"A ranger?"

"Yeah, you know how they get."

The Black Wolf motioned for James Lee to sit. James Lee squatted over a stool across from his boss.

"I'm tired of waiting for the break."

"These things take time."

"I have given time. Too much time."

"Once you make it out of here, we want it to stick, right?" The Black Wolf agreed. "Then we have to get everything in place. No mistakes. It won't be long now."

"No, it won't because I want it by next week."

"That's…that's impossible."

"I trust you."

He gave James Lee a sly grin.

"I can't be responsible if something happens on the way out."

"I'll worry about that."

James Lee knew arguing was pointless. He had a new deadline, months ahead of what he had been aiming toward. He knew he had to make it work, somehow.

"Roy tells me his wife talked to a ranger. Maybe the same one, maybe not. But I don't like it. I don't like it at all."

"His wife? What?"

"Talk to him about it. Doesn't sound good. I think you need to pay her a visit."

James Lee put another cigarette in his mouth and lit up. "Okay. I'll talk to him."

"Next week," The Black Wolf emphasized.

"Yeah. You'll be out, and we'll get you down across the border and screw this place."

"I trust you."

"I'll make it happen. Might cost, but I'll make it happen."

He blew a cloud of smoke that covered them both.

CHAPTER TWENTY-THREE

THE NEON SIGN SPUTTERED TO LIFE OUTSIDE THE MOTEL WHERE Concho was staying. Inside his room, he had gotten Maria on the phone, not knowing how she would be when he told her he wasn't coming home that night.

"It better be worth it," she said.

"So far I can't really tell. I got some good info, but the warden doesn't seem to want to investigate. He got a little pissed off when I suggested some of his men were on the take."

"Maybe he's in on it."

"Yeah, I thought that, but I don't know…"

Maria knew he was thinking of different angles, playing out scenarios. "So what next?"

"I'll see if there's anything else I can find out in the morning, otherwise I might need to turn it all over to Shaw and let the Rangers step in. Maybe there's something the prison board can do, but I'm not sure."

"I thought all you guys were on the same side."

"You'd think." He leaned back against the headboard and stretched his long legs out on the bed. "Most times, a whole lot could be solved if the different agencies just talked to each other more. You know how it goes."

"Yeah, pissing contest. What you need are more women in there. You know how they love to talk and share stories."

He chuckled. "Now if I'd said that…"

"You'd be a big ol' male chauvinist."

"Either way, I'll be home tomorrow. I promise."

"Okay." She sighed. "The girl is doing well. Anxious to get home to her parents, though."

"I get it."

"I would be too. All that kid has been through…it's a damn ugly world sometimes."

"Uglier for some."

Maria didn't respond. She didn't have to. Truth was truth and didn't need to be agreed with.

"Love you, baby," he said.

"Love you, sugar."

Maria made a kissing sound and then they hung up.

Concho thought about dinner, but he had plenty on his mind so he figured he'd just head back to the diner and maybe talk to June again. First, he called Shaw and filled him in.

"Let me ask around," Shaw said. "See if I know anyone who's had interactions with this Scalise. I'll find out if he's trustworthy."

"Okay, sounds good. I'm torn on trying to visit this Black Wolf myself, but after the brush-off I got from the warden, I didn't want to push it."

"Better if he's not on high alert anyway. You don't want to spook him."

"Yeah, you're probably right."

"Okay, see you back here tomorrow?"

"Yes, sir. Thanks for letting me come up here."

"Not a problem. The marshals said you had quite a time."

Concho smiled, thinking back to the wild chase. "You could say that."

"Sounds like you saved the day."

"Just offered a helping hand, is all."

"Well, it made the trip worth it so that makes me look good. See you back here tomorrow."

"Right."

Concho hung up and rolled off the bed. He went to the tiny bathroom and splashed water on his face, tried to clear his mind so he could start fresh and come up with a new angle for how to nail The Black Wolf with these crimes. He had no smoking gun, so far.

He let the water run in the sink and closed his eyes. He tried to imagine the water was a river running nearby. He searched his mind for memories of nature, for a connection to the land he could draw on. He needed to reset and to be cleansed so he could think on this fresh.

He wanted some sage to burn, the wise words of his grand-mother, Esadowa, or his friend and shaman, Meskwaa. He needed voices of ancestors and those wiser than himself to clear his mind and invite new ideas and thoughts, and he needed all of it before any more girls were hurt.

He stood there, eyes closed, for five minutes, but the ances-tors did not speak to him. The river never came. It was only ever a ring-stained sink and fluorescent lighting. Nature was far from this place, and he was far from finding the answers he sought.

* * *

CONCHO TOOK A SEAT AT THE COUNTER OF THE DINER. Business was booming compared to the first time he was here. Three booths taken, four seats at the counter. The one waitress on duty, Jean-Marie, the owner's wife, was running ragged. Obviously she was not used to this kind of work and plates were piled up at the pass-through window, coffee was burning in the pots, and dirty dishes were stacked at the end of the counter.

She passed by Concho without acknowledging him on her way to bring a plate of french fries to one of the booths.

Concho took his own menu from the holder and studied it looking for something better than the burger he'd had before.

Jean-Marie went behind the counter, stepped up to the pass-through window, and shouted, "Where's that goddamn chicken-fried steak?"

"Two minutes!" came the response from deep in the kitchen.

"You said that ten minutes ago."

She turned, blowing a strand of hair from her eyes, and noticed Concho.

"Great. One more."

"All alone?" he asked. Her exasperated look gave him the answer. "Where's June tonight?"

"A no-show. Great night for it. Everybody in town decided they didn't want to cook for themselves tonight."

Concho folded his menu and set it down on the counter. "Well, don't let me add to your stress. I'll find another option."

He stood and gave her a nod and a smile.

She didn't have a smile in her to give. "Your stomach will thank you."

She turned and grabbed another plate and practically threw it at a man sitting at the counter.

Concho stepped outside and made a phone call. With his cell he called the ranger station and asked for June's address.

CHAPTER TWENTY-FOUR

WARM BLOOD STILL LEAKED OUT OF JUNE'S NECK. JAMES LEE Morris hated knife work, but it was quieter than a gun. Quieter, but not cleaner. Not by a long shot.

He stood with one foot propped on the kitchen counter, water running in the sink and a wad of paper towels in his hand working at a smear of blood on his favorite boots. He wasn't worried about the trail of evidence the blood would mean, he just didn't want the leather ruined.

It hadn't been hard to get into her home. The locks were old and the front door warped. Most of the run-down house seemed like it had been wet at one point and then dried out, leaving a slightly musty smell to the wood. Now the smell of fresh blood filled the room as the pool of slow-moving red spread out from the long neck wound.

June's eyes were open and a slightly surprised look still hung on her face, but her muscles slowly relaxed as the last of the life drained from her.

James Lee had questioned her for quite a while—until he was satisfied she was telling the truth about what she had told the ranger. It accounted for the smaller cuts on her cheeks and nose and the duct tape pinning her to the chair that fell with her when she tipped after the fatal knife cut. That last spasm of an attempt to pull away from what she knew was coming.

Whether anything she said could come back to bite them, he wasn't sure yet. But it wasn't good news. Moving up the prison break plan was a good move all around, despite the extra effort it would take on his part.

There was always a part of him, too, that wondered if he had enough stashed away. If he should just look the other way once and let The Black Wolf get what's coming to him. If the break doesn't go well and The Black Wolf fails to make it out, a situation where the only other option is death, would that be so bad?

James Lee could take his cash reserves and get out, not look back. But how much is enough? Get The Black Wolf over the border and there is a bonus in it for James Lee. He knows this. He has planned for it. It is enough to keep him loyal for another week at least.

He tore off a fresh paper towel, leaving the roll down to only the brown cardboard tube, and dabbed at the spot on his boots. It looked like they wouldn't stain.

He rinsed the knife in the sink and slid it back into the scabbard when he heard tires crunching on the gravel outside.

* * *

CONCHO PARKED HIS TRUCK IN FRONT OF A SMALL ONE-STORY house that had seen better days. He hadn't expected much from a minimum-wage waitress in a small Texas town and this place matched exactly what he had in mind.

Her car, a sun-faded Geo Metro, sat in front of the house. Several lights were on inside giving the place a dull yellow glow. He stood for several moments and took it in. He listened. He looked.

Concho moved toward the door. He reached down and unclasped the snap on the holster hanging from his right hip. He let his palm rest on the butt of the gun there.

"June?"

He heard the creak of a floorboard and then the slap of a screen door in back. Concho rushed the front door and went through.

He smelled the blood first. With his Colt out in front of him like a dog sniffing the air, he cleared the room side to side. Then he let himself look down at June's body still taped to the chair and nearly empty of blood. A rug had soaked up most of it, but the pool was wide and moving slowly wider.

He didn't have time to take in the scene. He could see through the narrow house to the screen door he had just heard slam shut. He ran.

The backyard was dark. The lot butted up against some trees and the yard was fenced in on all sides by a crumbling wooden fence around six feet tall. Several boards were missing or leaning at angles.

Concho swept the yard with his eyes and the gun but saw nothing.

A fence board gave a small creak and fell out of place to the ground as if someone had just pushed it aside and let it swing. He ran in that direction.

* * *

From the way she described him, this had to be the ranger. In a way, it was good for James Lee to see him because it confirmed that her confession had been truthful before her death.

He stayed low in the neighbor's yard, a disused riding mower provided a little cover. He could see through the gap in the fence he'd just come through toward the tall ranger with the long hair. He saw the barrel of the Colt .45 in his hand. James Lee had ignored the knife and taken up his own gun. A few shots fired now might save his life and he could deal with the noise in that case.

He was reluctant to move. The tall, un-mown grass would

make noise and give him away if he ran. He waited for the ranger to see nothing in the yard and go back inside to deal with the waitress, but instead he came charging toward the hole in the fence.

James Lee Morris had no choice but to run.

* * *

CONCHO SAW MOVEMENT. GETTING HIS BIG BODY THROUGH THE gap in the fence wasn't a quick move. A nail dug into his shoulder as he turned sideways and squeezed through. He made a mental note to check when his last tetanus shot had been.

The neighbor's yard was a wasteland of used equipment, rusty tools and cases of empty beer bottles all drowning in a tangle of overgrown weeds and grass. He saw the figure move on the far side of the lawn. One man, at least for now. He kept his senses tuned, listening for more.

The man ran past three rusted propane cans in a pyramid and up the three steps to the back door. He led with his shoulder and went through the door like it was nothing more than a beaded curtain.

The killer was now inside another house. Concho noticed a rusty swing set in the yard and several old bicycles and a trike. He hoped they were in such sad shape because any kids who lived here were long gone.

Concho charged for the door.

* * *

JAMES LEE TRIPPED OVER THE PIECES OF THE BROKEN DOOR AND went to his knees. The house was equally narrow as June's and he had landed right in the living room. The furniture was old and out of style, the carpet stained and pocked with small cigarette burn marks. The walls were yellowed with decades of nicotine stains. On the wall hung a new flat-screen TV. One indulgence in a room that hadn't seen any other updates in quite a while.

On the TV was pornography playing at a very high volume. On the orange and green floral couch was a rather heavy-set and very startled couple in the midst of making love.

James Lee looked at them and then quickly looked away, not out of modesty but from disgust. He got to his feet and ran for the front door. He used the knob this time and left the door hanging open as he went through.

* * *

CONCHO WAITED OUTSIDE THE BROKEN BACK DOOR. HE DIDN'T want to charge into an ambush. He pressed his back against the side of the house, then pivoted with his gun leading the way inside. He didn't see the man he was after, but saw a whole lot more than he bargained for.

By now the couple had stood from the couch, undressed and confused. The porn on the TV still continued.

The woman saw Concho's gun and let out a yelp. She moved behind her partner who was quickly losing the mood.

"Where?" Concho said.

The man pointed toward the open front door. Concho went for the opening.

A shot hit the side of the house and Concho dove for the grass. Inside the woman screamed again.

Concho rolled and came up pointing his gun into the night but he was so surrounded by tall grass he could barely see. At least it would keep him covered.

He could faintly hear boots quickly hammering the pavement and getting farther away. Concho got to one knee and tried to see his prey ahead of him. Porch lights weren't enough to illuminate the street so he couldn't see anything more than a blur as the man ran away.

Concho dug himself out of the tall grass and began

moving along the pathway toward the street. He heard a car start and took off in a sprint.

Ahead, he saw taillights come on. The car faced away from him. He tried to get close enough to read the plates, but in the dim light and with his legs and arms pumping, he couldn't see it clearly. Tires squealed as the car jerked away from the curb. Concho fired two shots, aimed between the red taillights. He thought he heard one puncture the metal of the car, but the car did not slow.

All he could tell was that the car was a silver color and a big V-8. He thought possibly a Dodge Charger or a Challenger. Something new and not cheap. And something with a new hole in the trunk.

Concho slowed his pace and came to a stop in the middle of the street. He panted for breath and let the Colt dangle at his side. He looked around him at the other houses. Nobody else emerged from the shadows. If the man had taken off, most likely it meant nobody was with him. Nobody out here, at least. Concho felt certain this had been ordered by a man behind bars in cell block two.

He holstered his gun and turned back toward June's house.

CHAPTER TWENTY-FIVE

HE STAYED A GOOD PORTION OF THE NIGHT ANSWERING questions from the police and filling them in on what he'd been up to since he arrived in town. They came and took photos, wrote down descriptions of the car, went over the events as Concho told them three times with breaks in between when Concho could sit and wonder if June's death had been his fault.

He hadn't told anyone that she had spoken with him. Perhaps they had been seen together. It was a small town after all. A company town and the company was the prison. If someone associated with the prison had seen them talking and then brought that information to the right people, then maybe...?

But she had offered the information. He hadn't coerced her or used his authority as a ranger to get her to talk. She wanted it known. And now she was dead for it.

It would go down as a simple home invasion, likely motive as robbery. All it took was one look around this divorced waitress's home to know there was nothing worth stealing there. Concho gave them info, but held back some of his suspicions. If the local police took action on his theories and speculations and accused anyone and it turned out not to be true, then Concho would look like a fool and so would the Rangers by association.

The police interviewed the neighbors who had gotten dressed since the incident. They corroborated Concho's telling of the chase and the shot fired. Deputies dug a slug out of the wall of the house. Someone took a photo of a tire mark where the shooter had driven away, but Concho knew nothing would come of that.

Finally they released him and as he got into his truck, he saw the coroner rolling a gurney out the front door with a black body bag on top. He spoke to himself, nearly silent, a short prayer in the Kickapoo tongue. A blessing for June as she passed between worlds. A hope for peace for her spirit in the next phase.

* * *

Despite the late hour of the night before, Concho woke early. He called in to Shaw and told him of his night and what he had handed over to the local police.

"I guess this is their case now," he said.

"I agree with you," Shaw said. "The Black Wolf has to be involved in this somehow."

"I got nothing to pin on him, though. He's smoke. Can't get a hold on anything."

"If they find the person who murdered this woman it will lead to him, no doubt."

"I hope so."

"Anyway, you're on your way back?"

"Yeah. Be there in a few hours."

He waited to call Maria. Explaining his last few days would be easier in person, and there was much she didn't need to know.

* * *

THERE IS NOTHING LIKE A TEXAS HIGHWAY FOR THINKING. Long, straight, and with little to look at on either side beyond dull, flat scrub brush. Your own mind is your best companion.

Concho tried to think where he could have slipped and let June's name out there. He didn't think he did. The trouble with any informant is that by their nature they like to talk. June must have said something herself that got the target put on her back. Still, if Concho hadn't shown up at her diner in the first place, she'd still be alive.

He clicked on the radio to try to clear the guilty thoughts from his head, but it didn't help.

CHAPTER TWENTY-SIX

WHEN HE RETURNED TO EAGLE PASS, CONCHO DROVE straight to see Meskwaa. The modest and weather-beaten trailer just off the road always reminded Concho of the man himself. It had seen many days and nights, endured dry heat and soaking wetness, been tanned and faded by the sun and kept a firm footprint on the land. Meskwaa had been around for years, exactly how many nobody was sure, but he was both rooted in the land and as light as the wind that blew the dust across the flat plains.

Before Concho had turned off the engine, the old man appeared in the doorway of the trailer, a cigarette pinched between his thumb and forefinger, nearly smoked down to the skin on his hand.

Concho waved and Meskwaa nodded once, flicked the butt into the sand and turned inside, leaving the door open for Concho.

The midday sun was high overhead as Concho unfolded himself from behind the wheel. He hadn't stopped on the way home and his joints and muscles were stiff from the drive and the sprinting the night before. He stopped to have a stretch

before he went inside. A thin sweat had broken out on his forehead by the time he passed through the doorway.

"I saw a river," Meskwaa said. He sat in a chair, still as a
tree. "The river was red."

"I've had quite a time the past few days."

"I can read it on your face. Soon you will have lines as deep
as my own. The worry cuts into you like the river carves the
land."

"I don't doubt it." Concho sat and let out a long exhale.
The lack of sleep caught up with him in a rush. "A woman
died and I fear it is my fault."

"Did she die by your hand?"

"No. Not directly. But I think she died because she talked
to me."

"Did she talk willingly?"

"Yes."

Meskwaa nodded once slowly. "Look at your hands."

Concho did, holding them up in front of him.

"Do you see blood?" Meskwaa asked.

"No," Concho answered.

"But there was blood? The blood of this woman?"

"Yes. She was cut across the throat."

"But the blood does not stain your skin. You are not
responsible."

Concho let his hands fall into his lap. He felt marginally
better, but the guilt was still there.

"I know when I bring the man responsible to justice then I
will feel better."

Meskwaa reached for a cigarette from a small pouch made
of deerskin. He drew out an unfiltered cigarette and took some
time to study it in his hand. "But she will still be dead. Is it her
spirit or your own you wish to calm?"

"Both, I guess."

Meskwaa lit the cigarette and drew a deep lungful of
smoke, then let it out to swirl around him.

"I did not know the river vision was about you, Ten-Wolves. If there was blood, perhaps I should have."

"That's not good when any vision of death makes you think of me."

"History has proven itself, hasn't it?"

Concho chuffed out a small laugh. Meskwaa wasn't wrong.

"Have you seen anything else lately?" Concho asked the elder.

Meskwaa thought, letting the smoke rise and dissipate. "Not of violence. Some of fear. But fear is all around us."

"Like what?"

"I have seen a wolf running. Running as the sunlight fades and it turns to night."

Concho leaned forward. "What color was the wolf?"

Meskwaa could see his intrigue. "Black. Same as the night it seemed to run toward."

"Was anyone chasing the wolf?"

"Perhaps you?"

Concho nodded. Meskwaa shook his head. "I saw only the wolf. It ran into the setting sun and then was swallowed up. But a wolf runs for only two reasons."

"Such as?"

"To hunt, or if it is being hunted."

Concho settled back in his chair. He leaned his head back and closed his eyes.

"Does this wolf have meaning to you?" Meskwaa asked.

"Yes. Only I don't know yet if I am the hunter or the hunted."

Concho drifted to sleep.

CHAPTER TWENTY-SEVEN

Unlike Concho, James Lee Morris slept in late, Most of the day, actually. When he got home from the close call at June's house, he'd poured himself a stiff drink. Then another. His nerves were open live wires, his hands shaky. He needed the drinks to calm him and not feel like the tall ranger was right outside his window.

James Lee knew the one shot he took hadn't hit anything but the siding of the cheap house, but he needed the cover to reach his car. He felt fairly sure the ranger hadn't seen him enough to ID him, but he couldn't be sure at all what June had told him.

She named the ranger—Concho Ten-Wolves, which James Lee thought was a lie at first. A silly name, but now that he had seen the man himself, maybe it was true. He would have to make some calls to check up.

When he finally dragged himself from bed he was sweating in his sheets from the midday sun coming in through the window. He showered in cold water until he felt half human and then ate a big plate of eggs, bacon, and toast with butter. He drank three glasses of orange juice to rehydrate.

He made a choice not to call over to Bigfoot and report

what had happened to The Black Wolf. The man kept his nose in too much of James Lee's business as it was. For someone locked behind bars, he sure was an imposition on James Lee's day-to-day life.

He called one of his hired men, Toby. Toby was thick in an ex-high school linebacker way. That was all the football and all the education the man ever got. He came cheap and was lazy in all other areas of his life, but when it came to intimidation and cracking heads, you couldn't do any better than Toby. It seemed to be the only thing he enjoyed in life, scaring people and breaking fingers, legs, kneecaps. James Lee had used him on a killing once, but it wasn't Toby's specialty. Brute force, that was his game.

He met the tough man at a coffee shop and James Lee ordered a large black coffee. He needed the extra jolt. He put Toby in the passenger seat of his car and made his way to his meeting.

Warden Frank Scalise didn't know he had a meeting with James Lee. He thought he was coming home to dinner with his wife like any other night.

James Lee and Toby arrived at the warden's home before Scalise got there. His wife, Debra, answered the door. A plump woman with a smile on her face like a golden retriever, she opened the door wide and said, "Yes. May I help you?"

Toby pushed inside and knocked her over with the door. Her smile faded away.

They waited nearly an hour. Debra sat on the sofa in the modest living room. Everything tidy and in its place. Family photos showed the Scalise's and their two grown kids at national parks, a Dallas Cowboys game and a rodeo. A framed painting of Jesus watched silently on the wall, a glow emanating from his heart as he ignored the threat to Debra, His devoted servant.

James Lee was still thirsty somehow. He went into the kitchen and found a pitcher of iced tea and was on his third glass when the warden came home.

Frank Scalise stopped in the doorway, his key still in the lock. He saw the hulking figure of Toby sitting in his chair across from his wife and James Lee standing nearby looking like he had just popped in for a visit after church.

Scalise knew James Lee from his time as a guard. After he quit, James Lee came back for a visit to let him know Henna worked for The Black Wolf and that if Scalise wanted to maintain order in his prison, he needed to look the other way on a few things. A few became a few hundred, but there was peace within the walls and Scalise found it a worthy compromise. The warden had never taken any money from the cartel, but he knew enough about when to turn a blind eye. If anything, keeping The Black Wolf happy kept things running smoothly at the facility so that the warden didn't feel like it was a dereliction of duty.

But an unannounced visit to his home—this couldn't be good.

"What are you doing here?" the warden said.

"Come in," James Lee said. "Take off your coat. Let's talk."

Scalise shut the door and made eye contact with his wife. He could see the fear in her eyes, but she looked unharmed. Just scared.

He set down his briefcase and his jacket on the entry table and put his keys in the bowl. He waited for instructions.

"Come on in. Sit, sit." James Lee gestured to the spot next to Debra on the sofa.

The warden moved slowly to the spot and took his wife's hand as he sat.

"You okay?" he said quietly to her.

Debra nodded and whispered, "Who are these men?"

Scalise realized he didn't know who Toby was, but he didn't like the look of him. And if he came with James Lee, he wasn't on their side.

"It'll be okay. Just relax."

James Lee swallowed the last of the iced tea in his glass and set it down on a side table. Scalise felt Debra shift as she watched the sweating glass go down on the wood without a coaster, but he squeezed her hand to let her know they had more important issues in front of them right then.

"I understand you had a visitor," James Lee said.

Scalise thought hard about who he could mean.

James Lee clarified. "A Texas Ranger."

It clicked. The tall black man with the long straight hair. Two-Wolves or something like that. The one making accusations about The Black Wolf.

"I didn't tell him anything," Scalise said.

"Well, I guess that settles it." James Lee gave a big smile. He turned to address Toby. "What do you think, Toby? Should we trust him that he kept his mouth shut?"

"I don't trust nobody about nothing."

James Lee settled on the arm of the sofa near Frank. "Maybe we should ask for a little more than just your word for it."

"Do you think I'm a fool?" Scalise said. "He came in asking about all sorts of things that y'all are doing and I kicked him out. It's not me you need to be worried about. If the damn Rangers are onto you, there's not a damn thing I can do about it."

"Okay, so let's say that you didn't tell him anything. What did he want to know?"

"He knew about the girls." Scalise felt the cold stare of his wife beside him. Debra had been ignorant of all that went on with The Black Wolf up at the prison. Frank didn't want to spill too much, but he certainly wanted to do or say anything that would avoid spilling any blood.

"They got your guys coming across down south," he said. "That led him up here. The problem isn't with me, it's with your other men."

"If there's a problem, it concerns all of us."

"Look, James, you know me. When you worked for me, did I make a fuss? Did I tell anybody anything I wasn't supposed to? It's been nearly ten years and I've kept my mouth shut. And I never took a dime from y'all. All I do is keep my business to myself and let y'all do the same. That's gotta earn some trust, hasn't it?"

James Lee thought about it.

Toby leaned forward, hands on his knees. "Man has a real hard time lying when I'm about to bust his fingers."

Debra makes a small noise of fear in her throat. Frank squeezed her hand tighter. "You don't need to do that. I didn't tell him anything."

James Lee held out a calming hand. "Okay. I'm on your side here, Scalise. I want to believe you. What I also want is for you to believe me when I tell what the consequences are if you start talking."

"Oh, I know. I do."

"Do you? I'm not so sure." James Lee stood. "You see, that ranger might come back. He might send someone else. You might start to feel pressure. But I can assure you, the pressure you feel up in your cushy office is nothing compared to what you'll feel on the outside if I think you're talking to them."

"I know, I swear I know."

James Lee turned to Debra. "Do you know? I want to make sure you're not one of those people who wants your husband to do the right thing at all costs. Because, trust me, lady, you don't want to suffer the costs here. Because it's pay with your life."

"I..." Debra cleared her throat. "I understand."

He held her gaze for a long moment, looking for any weakness. Finally he clapped his hands once. "Okay. I think you get the point. And listen, if someone does come back—same guy or not – I want to know about it. I want to know all the details. You got a recorder in that office of yours?"

"No."

"Dumb. You should. Well, you better hope you remember every syllable of every word they say if they come back, because I'm gonna want to know it."

"I won't say a word. I promise."

James Lee stood over them and put his hands on his hips. "Y'know, you weren't such a bad boss. Spineless, weak. But not bad." He turned to Toby.

"He's gonna want to know we were here."

Scalise knew who the "he" was. The Black Wolf.

Toby reached into the pocket of his light coat and removed a long pair of shears. Frank and Debra both tensed on the sofa.

"Please," Frank said. "You don't have to do anything like that. I promised. I told you everything that happened. I didn't lie, I didn't hide anything. You gotta trust me."

"What do you think is gonna happen now?" He looked between Toby and the Scalise's on the sofa. "You think, what, I'm gonna have Toby cut off one of your fingers?"

Toby stood. The shears were long and silver, the kind tailors use.

James Lee crouched in front of the couple, got eye level with them for the first time.

"Is that what you think? I'm gonna take your pinky finger and show it to the boss so he knows we were here?"

He turned to Debra. "Maybe hers is better. Make you understand that I'm not just talking about you here. You got two kids, too. Not hard to find. Between all of them, that's a lot of fingers."

"Please," Scalise said quietly, pleading.

A tear fell down Debra's cheek.

James Lee reached out and touched her hand. She flinched away from him. He held her hand in place, then ran his fingers along her index finger.

"Which one would be best? Which one makes the point? Do you take something she needs every day?"

He moved his hand over to her middle finger.

"Does that make the point?"

He ran his fingertips gently along her ring finger, touching the tiny diamond in her engagement ring. Nothing more than a chip. Barely reflected any light.

"Or do you take the smallest one? Just a reminder. That way she knows she had more to lose if you screw up."

He touched her pinky finger. Debra's hands trembled now.

"Hard decision, isn't it?"

"You don't have to do this," Scalise said.

"Is that really what you think of me? This is what you think we'd do?" James Lee stood quickly. "We're not animals, Frank. We want to work *with* you. There may come a time very soon when I need your discretion. I want you to remember this moment when that time comes. I don't want to come begging. I want you to be agreeable."

He flicked his wrist and called Toby over. Toby leaned forward and brought the shears up to Debra's face. She closed her eyes and let loose a tiny whimper. As she closed her eyes, she squeezed out more tears.

Toby reached for a lock of her graying hair behind her ears and snipped off an inch-long piece. He pocketed the shears and brought out a plastic bag, placed the lock of hair inside and sealed it.

"See?" James Lee said. "We're reasonable people."

Debra opened her eyes. She saw the small curl of hair inside the bag and touched behind her ear where she had felt the snip.

"Nothing to say?" James Lee said.

"Thank you," Scalise said.

"There you go. Okay, we're outta here. It's been lovely. Hope to see you again."

He waved Toby toward the door, and they both walked out calmly as Debra collapsed into her husband's arms, weeping.

CHAPTER TWENTY-EIGHT

Concho stopped at the office to see Shaw before he went home. He'd called Maria when he finally awoke at Meskwaa's and told her would be home soon. He needed to fill in his boss in person.

Company D had been quiet the past few days, so Dalton Shaw had time. He listened to the re-telling in Concho's own words, feeling a small pang of regret he hadn't seen the action himself.

"Sounds like a hell of a time," Shaw said.

"And now a woman is dead because of me."

"No, don't do that," Shaw cautioned. "You were doing your job. Nothing more."

Concho shifted uncomfortably in his seat.

"You think the locals up there can handle it?" Shaw asked.

"I doubt they'll find the killer. This was no robbery or home invasion. He was sent by The Black Wolf or someone associated with him. As far as the local police doing anything about The Back Wolf that they haven't done in nine years already…I'm not holding my breath."

"Hmm, yeah."

Shaw lifted a file folder from his desk. "Well," he said, "the good news is the girl has been released by ICE. She can go home to Mexico."

"Really? That's great."

Shaw dropped the folder on his desk so Concho could pick it up. He waited while the gears turned in Concho's head.

"Do you think I could escort her home?" he asked.

Commander Shaw smiled. "I was wondering how long it would take you to get there."

"Sir?"

"I already approved it and cleared your schedule."

"Thank you."

"Like you did up north, I want you to make the most of this. Find out what you can, but try to stay out of trouble south of the border, okay, Ten-Wolves?"

"I'll do my best."

"Do better than that. I don't want to have to get any angry calls from the federales about you shooting up their jurisdiction."

"You won't. I swear."

Shaw gave him a dubious smile. "Yeah, I wish that was worth the air it took you to say it. Just do your best."

"I will."

Concho stood and brought the file with him as he exited.

* * *

MARIA GRABBED HIM TIGHTLY AND KISSED HIM WITH AN OPEN mouth and probing tongue. He bent down and lifted her. When they broke, she said, "About time."

Concho set her down. "I bring good news."

"What is it?"

"Ximena can go home."

"Oh, great."

Maria called to her. Once again, Ximena was in the kitchen. The smells of spicy food and fresh tortillas filled the house.

She came to meet them, wiping her hands on an improvised apron made from a small towel.

"Concho says you can go home."

He held up the file.

"Approved this morning."

Ximena smiled and brought her hands together in prayer.
She spoke rapid-fire Spanish, then switched to English to thank
them both. She moved back into the kitchen, light on her feet,
to finish cooking.

"Now, for the other news," Concho said. "Which is either
good news or bad news depending on which one of you I'm
talking to."

Maria folded her arms in front of her. "Uh-oh."

"I'm escorting Ximena back home. While I'm there, I'm
going to ask around and get some information. Might take a
day or two."

Maria looked annoyed. "Y'know I dated a truck driver
once. I hated how he was gone all the time. Plus, he never got
shot at."

"This is a special circumstance, you know that. I'll see that
she gets home safe and find out a little more for the case."

"You close to busting this bastard?"

"Closer. Hard to find a direct connection, though. That's
why it needs some more legwork."

"I could use a little of that, myself."

She studied him to make sure he knew what she meant.
He did.

"I promise once I get back, we'll have the whole place to
ourselves. maybe I'll even ask Shaw for a few days off."

"Seems like you've been out of the office enough these
days."

"For work, Maria. These aren't vacations."

"I hope not."

He stepped close to her and put a hand on her arm.
"When I was up near the prison, a woman died. She had given
me information and I think she died because of it."

"Oh my god. Concho, I'm so sorry."

"I wouldn't go if I didn't think I needed to. But I need to make sure there are no other girls like Ximena crossing the border, and I want to make sure this Black Wolf pays for these crimes."

"Of course." She stood on her toes and kissed him again. "You go do what you need to."

They embraced. Concho smelled the food cooking again. "You pick up any tips while she's been here?"

She broke the embrace and gave him a hard stare. "My cooking is just fine, thank you very much."

"I'm just saying. It smells good."

"It tastes good too. She's been doing nothing but cooking since she got here. Maybe when she gets home, they'll make you a feast to celebrate."

"You know I love your cooking."

"Don't try to save it now, mister." She playfully poked him in the chest. "You can make it up to me when you get back, and we're alone again."

"Now THAT I can promise you do better than anyone else."

"Oh, you better not have that much information to compare me to." She pushed him away with a smile. "But you're right, you know." Maria winked.

CHAPTER TWENTY-NINE

XIMENA HAD NO LUGGAGE, JUST A FEW NEW OUTFITS MARIA had bought her at the mall or taken from lost and found. Those she kept in a grocery bag that she set on the seat between her and Concho in the cab of his truck. Concho stopped on the porch for a long kiss with Maria, then got behind the wheel to bring Ximena back home.

She eyed his dual revolvers as he got in. He saw her eyes trace over the guns.

"It's okay," he said. "I don't anticipate trouble. It's my job to wear them."

She nodded her approval, but it was unconvincing.

The trip to the border from Eagle Pass was short. The Rio Grande flowed only minutes south of them. Concho made his way to the Camino Real International Bridge and showed his ID and his ranger badge to the border guards there. He had a letter of passage from ICE with Ximena's information and the approval to bring her home. After a cursory scrutiny of the documents, they let him pass and they entered Piedras Negras on the Mexican side of the border.

Concho always marveled how a thin strip of water could separate two different worlds. Many of the houses on the

Mexican side seemed made of temporary material, as if no one expected to occupy them for very long. There were lovely houses nearby in the state of Coahuila, large haciendas with swimming pools and courtyards. The Kickapoo people and indigenous Mexicans did not live in these fine homes.

Concho turned east, drove along dry dirt roads following the directions he'd been given to Ximena's home. After a long stretch of nothing, they came to a dense patch of one-story homes. Shades of brown, red clay, and tan on all the structures leaning a little in one direction or the other, like the wind had blown them sideways. There were no green lawns, no town square. It was quite easy to see how young people in an area like this could be tempted into working for the cartels who promised money and clothing and possessions they would never hope to have if they stayed living the life of the forgotten.

Ximena bounced in her seat and pointed to a turn ahead. She was already crying as they drove past homes with broken fences and open doors. It may not have been much, but it was home to this girl and she was happy to be back.

"*Aqui, aqui,*" she said, pointing to a large Dodge pickup parked beside a house in faded green.

Concho eased his truck to a stop and she got out before the wheels had stopped turning. Ximena shouted for Mama and Papa as she ran toward the house. Concho watched as her mother was first out the door and the two embraced, clutching each other tightly to the point it looked like they would break bones.

Ximena's father appeared in the doorway with a hand over his mouth and tears flowing freely down his face. He stood and watched his wife and daughter embrace and sobbed at the sight.

Concho stayed by his truck and let the family reunite. Neighbors began coming out onto their front porches and yards to witness the miracle. Concho heard prayers of thanks in Spanish being made by the women.

After several minutes, when the family seemed cried out, the father turned to Concho and walked to him, his hand outstretched to shake the hand of the man who brought his daughter home to him.

"*Gracias, mi amigo. Te agradezco de corazón.*"

Concho shook the man's hand and said, "*De nada.*"

He was invited in for food and drinks.

The afternoon became a fiesta. The whole neighborhood turned out, it seemed. Concho drank a Fanta and smiled at the happy faces of the people who had thought they lost another of their own, but got one back who they all considered a daughter now.

Concho didn't press, but he asked questions of the people he found who spoke English.

"How many girls have been taken from your town?"

A man in a sweat-stained cowboy hat shook his head ruefully, "Too many, *señor.* Ximena was the ninth one. But the first to come back to us." He lifted his beer bottle to toast the miraculous good fortune.

"And the local authorities can't do anything to stop it?"

"The federales?" He coughed out a laugh. "They get paid *mucho dinero* to look away. *Mucho.*"

Later, he found a woman standing alone and spoke with her.

"Are all the girls that are taken native girls?"

"*Sí.*"

So far the stories all corroborated what June had told him, but he wasn't getting much new information.

The woman studied Concho. "And you...you are...?"

"Kickapoo," he said. "With West African mixed in."

She said, "Ahhh," as if a great secret had been revealed.

"And you brought our Ximena back to us?"

"Yes, I did." He showed his badge. "Texas Ranger."

The woman leaned forward and kissed him on the cheek. "*Gracias.*"

"Yes, ma'am." He finished the last of his drink. "May I ask you, have you heard the name The Black Wolf? *El Lobo Negro?*"

Her face went dark. "Sí."

"And is he involved in the disappearances?"

"*El lobo negro es el diablo.* He's the devil, Mr. Concho."

"But he is in jail."

"You can put an animal in the zoo, but he can still bite."

* * *

A SKINNY YOUNG MAN, ONLY NINETEEN, WAS LINGERING ON THE fringes of the party. A local boy, nobody paid him any mind. He drank a beer but didn't look to be celebrating. He kept an eye on the American, studying him. He saw him flash his ranger badge to Yesenia. The skinny boy drained the last of his beer and left the party.

CHAPTER THIRTY

THE SKINNY BOY BROKE INTO A RUN AS SOON AS HE LEFT BEHIND the party. He was drenched in sweat when he reached the house on the far side of town. Another anonymous tan adobe structure, this one had bars on the windows and a barricaded door in front as well as hidden security cameras up under the eaves. He knocked on the front door and waited, panting for breath.

Inside, Mateo checked the monitor. It was Cedro, the skinny kid who joined the crew a year ago. He'd been eager to do any job they threw his way. He wanted nothing more than to make money and get out, move to the States, and working for the cartel was his way north. The kid was sometimes too eager, though. Hard to keep his mouth shut and his size kept him from being intimidating in any way. He was doomed to be an errand boy unless he proved himself invaluably smart, which frankly hadn't happened yet.

Mateo buzzed the front door open and Cedro slumped in.

"Have you heard from Hugo or Rubén?" Cedro coughed into his fist, still trying to regain a normal breathing pattern.

"Not since they crossed north," Mateo said. "Why?"

"The girl is back. Ximena."

Mateo was confused. "You saw her?"

"They're having a party for her right now."

This didn't sit right with Mateo. The girls never came back. "Where?"

"Her house."

"And you were there?"

"Yes. She is my neighbor."

"What did she say? How?"

Cedro leaned against a long table in the entryway. "Can I get a glass of water or something?"

Annoyed, Mateo beckoned him to the kitchen where he poured him a glass of water. After Cedro eagerly drank it down without pausing, he drew a deep breath and then explained.

"Some American brought her back over. A Texas Ranger. Everyone was saying he rescued her."

Mateo thought about it. "This must be why Hugo asked for another girl so soon after. I thought it was too quick for another."

"Did you call them?"

"No. Maybe I will."

Mateo walked away to get his phone. Cedro sat in a kitchen chair and slowed his breathing. He fanned his shirt to dry the sweat.

* * *

HUGO AND RUBÉN HAD BEEN STUCK IN A MOTEL FOR TWO DAYS with the girl. When they got the call that The Black Wolf needed another, they didn't question it. When they took the girl from Mateo at the border, they didn't ask her name. They had done it before, and they knew they would do it again. Get the girl on the Mexican side, move her over, transfer her to Ricky and then come home to a payday waiting.

But Ricky hadn't shown. Something had gone wrong. Communication had been sparse but finally they got a call to just stay low and wait it out. Trouble with the Rangers. They needed to wait until the coast was clear, as they say in America.

The two men could have been brothers, many said. Same age, same size, same dark hair in the same slicked-back style. Hugo had one gold tooth that made him stand out, but otherwise they were the perfect pair since they were interchangeable. They moved mostly product over the border. They had crossed hundreds of times, moving millions in drugs. The women were only a tiny bit more complicated.

Hugo had grown bitter that the money he handed over to crooked border agents was more than what he got for the job, but he learned to live with it and each time he got home to a bundle of American dollars waiting for him, it took the sting off a little.

Rubén never questioned it. He counted his money, smoked his cigarettes, drank his tequila and did the job. Exactly the kind of mindless worker bee James Lee Morris liked to have on his team.

They'd stayed in this room of this motel a hundred times also. The owner took a much smaller roll of bills to look the other way.

The girl looked like a rag doll, half unstuffed and ignored. She knew as soon as they came for her what her fate would be. She'd heard the stories of the others. She knew they never come home. They had grabbed her before she heard about Ximena. Her only defense was to shut off, close down. Go limp.

Hugo's phone rang and he answered it.

"Sí?"

"Hugo? Mateo. Are you all right?"

"Yeah. Why?"

Mateo explained. Hugo explained back about being held up, about Ricky not showing up for the transfer, about being warned off the safe house on the Reservation.

"So what do we do?" Hugo asked.

"I don't know. We wait to find out, I guess."

"This is messed up," Hugo said. "I don't like it."

"Me neither. You hear from the *gringo*, James Lee?"

"Only to say stay low. I do what he says. He's *loco*."

"I know. Look, you hear anything, you call me."

"Okay. You do the same."

* * *

MATEO TAPPED THE PHONE AGAINST HIS LEG, THINKING.

"You gotta get over there, find out more about this guy who brought her back," he said to Cedro.

"Like what?"

"Like how much he knows. Is he down here to arrest people?"

"Okay, okay. I'll check it out."

Mateo could see the eager puppy dog in him perk up. He needed to warn him. "Yeah, but be subtle about it. Don't just walk up and start asking him questions, man. If he doesn't know about us, I don't want him to, you feel me?"

"Yeah, yeah, I feel you."

Mateo couldn't stop his swirling thoughts. None of it made sense. "Big man ain't gonna be happy."

"No way."

"Okay, go see what you can find out. Talk to the girl, too. You know her?"

"Yeah, since we were kids."

Mateo stopped and thought. "Did she see you when we snagged her?"

"Nah, man. She didn't recognize me through the masks."

"You sure?"

"Yeah, bro. I'm sure."

"Okay. 'Cause if you get pinned, it sure as hell is coming back on me. And I can't have that."

"None of us can, man."

Mateo went to the fridge for a beer. "I don't like it."

CHAPTER THIRTY-ONE

THE PARTY BEGAN TO WIND DOWN. CONCHO HAD FADED TO THE sidelines, letting the family reunite and the friends offer congratulations. He hadn't learned anything new, but he hadn't pushed it. He wanted to let the celebration play out before acting like a cop.

He noticed a woman also standing by herself on the opposite side of the yard. He could see she was upset. Tears ran slowly down her cheeks as she watched Ximena wrapped in hugs. Concho set down his beer and crossed the yard to her.

"You okay, ma'am?"

She wiped her face and tried to put on a smile.

"Yes, I'm sorry. I didn't want to ruin the party."

"It's okay. Is everything all right?"

"Don't misunderstand, I am thrilled for Ximena and for her parents. But it's just that..." She looked on the verge of tears again. "My Consuela was taken, too. I worry I won't be as lucky."

"Your daughter was taken? By the same people?"

She nodded. "Will you try to find her the same way you found Ximena?"

"I'll do what I can. When was she taken?"

"Three days ago."

Concho was stunned. He hadn't heard about it. It didn't fit the pattern for another girl to be taken so soon. There had been many months in between the others. But Ximena hadn't arrived at her destination. This other girl had probably been the replacement.

"And you've told the authorities?"

"Yes, but…" She stared down at the dirt, a more hopeless look Concho had never seen. He decided he needed to talk to the local federales and ask some questions. He guessed it was somewhat like the States and that girls from the Rez always took a lower priority.

"What is your name?" he asked her.

"Faustina."

"I'm Concho," he told her and reached out to take her hand. "I'll do what I can." She squeezed his hand hard and thanked him.

* * *

LONG AFTER DARK, THE LAST OF THE VISITORS WENT HOME. Ximena and her mother washed dishes and laughed with each other, playfully bumping hips and splashing in the sudsy water. They reveled in the simple chore neither of them thought they would get to share ever again.

Ximena's father, Alberto, brought Concho a bottle of beer and one for himself. He gestured for them to sit in cheap plastic chairs in the yard. Concho sat and they listened to the women, their voices like music in the night.

Alberto drank his *cerveza* and tilted his head back to the stars.

"The men who took my *hija*, did they come to justice?"

"The man I found her with did, yes."

"*Muerto?*"

"Yes, dead."

Alberto gave a satisfied nod and drank more.

"There is more to be done," Concho said. "Nobody down here knows who is taking the girls?"

"I'm sure people know. But they are too afraid or too well paid to speak up."

"*El Lobo Negro?*"

"Yes. The Black Wolf. But he is one of many who are ruining my country. But he came up through the locals. The natives. He is one of the tribe. He exploits his own people."

"They all do. Doesn't matter what you look like or where your ancestors come from."

Alberto gave a sad tilt of his head. "This is true."

"Do you think you can find anyone who will talk to me? To point me in the right direction?"

"This would be very dangerous for you. And for me."

Concho patted the guns on his hips. "I'm not worried."

"I am."

Concho stood. "I should get to my hotel. Thank you for your hospitality."

"Thank you, Concho, for bringing my daughter back to us."

"My goal is for no other families to go through the same ordeal."

"May the spirits guide you in your task."

They shook hands and Concho walked to his truck.

* * *

ALBERTO BROUGHT THE EMPTY BOTTLES TO THE TRASH CAN AND he stood listening to music float in from a house down the street. There was no moon so the stars were out in great numbers. He stared up at the pinpoints of light and the faded white band of the Milky Way overhead.

His daughter was home, but others were still missing. And only one man had come to justice, according to the ranger. One was not enough.

He heard movement and shut the lids on the trash cans so

the dogs couldn't get at them. Skinny hounds with patchy fur roamed the neighborhood living off scraps and handouts. Alberto felt like that was how they all lived here. There had been many times in his life he felt no different than a dog.

Out of the shadows stepped a man he recognized—Jaimie. He glanced furtively around them in search of prying eyes.

"Alberto," he said. The man was thin and his beard was patchy so he looked more like one of the dogs than just about anyone in the neighborhood.

"Jaime. *¿Cómo estás?*"

"I have information for you."

"Information about what?"

CHAPTER THIRTY-TWO

CONCHO CHECKED INTO HIS HOTEL ROOM. THE PLACE WAS A single row of concrete-walled rooms, dirty carpets and bent venetian blinds. He did some pushups, some sit-ups, and leg lifts, then took a shower with the lowest water pressure he'd ever felt.

This room had surely seen some unsavory things. Concho tried not to think about them. He wondered if any of the girls had been brought here as a stop-over before crossing north. He doubted it. Best thing would be to get them across soon. Once they entered the United States, they'd be impossible to find. Disappearing in a place as big as Texas wasn't that hard, in the end.

He was thirsty but resisted drinking the local tap water. He'd have to run out and get some bottles at the gas station down the road. He pulled on a shirt and was about to walk out when there was a knock at the door. An urgent knuckling in rapid time.

Concho lifted one of his Colts from the holster that sat on the side table.

He stepped away from the door, putting his body behind the concrete wall.

"Who is it?"

"Ximena."

He used one finger to move a slat in the blinds to the side and peer out. She appeared alone. He opened the door.

Ximena pushed inside.

"What is it?" he asked. "What's wrong?"

"My father. He has gone to find the men who kidnapped me."

"What do you mean?"

"Someone came to the house. A man from the neighborhood. He told my father he knew who had taken me and where they lived. Father went after them. He took a gun."

Concho strapped on his holster. "Can you show me where?"

* * *

ALBERTO KNOCKED ON THE DOOR WITH THE BUTT OF THE shotgun. He wore a navy blue bandana around the lower half of his face. He'd had one, maybe two too many beers and he knew it, but once he knew where the men who had taken Ximena lived, there was no waiting.

He hadn't had to go very far, and that disturbed him. Men from his own neighborhood, men who were part of his community, had been the ones to take his daughter and so many others. Alberto tightened his grip with both hands while he waited for the door to open.

Cedro answered, the skinny boy opening the door without concern. Alberto rammed the butt of the shotgun into his chest and pushed through the door.

Cedro fell back, air rushing from his lungs. He landed hard on the tile floor and Alberto was inside and shutting the door behind him.

Alberto swept the room with the gun while Cedro wheezed below. He went and stood over the skinny boy until he caught his breath.

"Are you the one?" he said.

"What are you talking about, man?" Cedro asked.

"Did you take my daughter?"

Alberto saw a moment flash over the young man's face. An admission written in fear. He pushed the barrel of the shotgun down into the boy's face, letting it hang there only an inch away from his skin.

"Did you?"

"Gimme a minute, man."

"A yes or no question."

"Look, look...wait."

Alberto pushed the gun lower until the cold steel pressed against Cedro's cheekbone. Despite the bandana, he recognized the old man. Ximena's father.

"I'm a runner, man. An assistant. I don't make the calls."

Alberto shoved and the metal bruised Cedro's skin. "Who does, then?"

"You know who."

"The Black Wolf."

Cedro moved his head in a tiny nod, careful not to upset the old man or make his finger jump on the trigger.

"He's in prison. In the States. Who makes the call down here? Not you. You're a child."

"There are guys."

"Take me to them."

"They'll kill you."

"They won't have the chance."

Alberto lifted his boot, set it down in the middle of Cedro's crotch, and slowly let his weight shift to that foot. Cedro grunted and tried to wriggle away, but the shotgun barrel kept him in place.

A floorboard creaked. A boom sounded that made Cedro think the shotgun had gone off, but his head was still in one piece. Mateo leaned around a doorway, his hand out and a pistol smoking at the end of it.

The shot had gone high, missing Alberto and smashing

into the plaster of the wall behind him. Alberto swung the shotgun up and centered it on the doorway. He fired. Mateo jumped backward with the impact, throwing his own gun as he flailed in reverse. He landed in a heap on the floor, his shirt dotted with blood.

Alberto kept one boot grinding into Cedro's crotch. He swung the shotgun back down to the young man's face. Cedro could feel the heat from the barrel.

"Who else is here?"

"Nobody! I swear."

Alberto ground his boot heel and asked again. "Who else?"

"No one."

Mateo groaned from the floor in the other room. He tried to move, but every motion was agony.

Alberto reached down and balled a fist of Cedro's shirt. He lifted the boy.

"Come with me."

Cedro got to his feet, the shotgun pressed against him.

"Show me these other men," Alberto said. "Take me to them."

"I can't do that, man."

Alberto pressed the shotgun barrel into his side. "Yes, you can." He tilted his head toward Mateo. "See him?" Cedro knew the old man was serious.

"Okay, all right. Jesus, man."

Alberto turned the boy toward the door. "You drive."

He shoved Cedro out in front of him. Alberto bent down and picked up the pistol from the floor where it had fallen and tucked it in his waistband. He left the door open as he pushed Cedro toward his truck. He made the boy get behind the wheel and he climbed in beside him, keeping the shotgun pointed at him the whole time.

"They'll kill you, old man."

"Not if I kill them first."

CHAPTER THIRTY-THREE

AN OPEN DOOR IS NEVER GOOD NEWS WHEN YOU ARRIVE ON A scene. Concho stepped out of his truck and immediately drew the Colt from his right hip. He leaned against the hood of the truck and let his eyes slowly scan the area. He saw no movement outside the house.

The low ranch-style home sat on a dirt patch well away from any other houses. In this area, land was plentiful and the homes spread out across the dusty landscape. Concho noticed the tire tracks of another truck which had been there recently. There hadn't been time for the wind to obscure the tracks in the blowing dust. He moved slowly toward the door, gun at the ready.

He listened at the door but heard nothing. The heavy security door moved slightly in the breeze, creaking on a hinge. He thought about sticking to protocol and calling out that he was a ranger, but he was well outside his jurisdiction so he didn't see the point. He stepped inside.

The unmistakable smell of a recently fired weapon hung in the air. Concho moved slowly through the entryway and into the main room. His feet were silent on the tiles. He stepped delicately like he was tracking an animal through the woods.

To his right he spotted a body. He approached cautiously, expecting to find Alberto. Instead it was a much younger man. As Concho got closer, he moved.

Concho could see blood on his shirt in a wide, spreading stain. The man let out a low moan and made small movements as if every motion hurt his whole body. Concho bent down close to him.

"Hello?"

The man grunted again.

"Is there a phone? I'll call you an ambulance."

The man's eyes came open. "*Americano?*"

"*Sí*"

"*Telefono…allí.*"

He lifted a weak hand and pointed where a wall-mounted phone hung. Concho went to it and called in help. He came back to the man and bent close to him.

"Was it Alberto?"

"*No se.*"

"Where did he go? *Donde?*"

Mateo looked down at his chest, pressed a hand into the pool of blood there and then looked at his palm.

"Shotgun," he said. "He took Cedro."

"Who did?"

"Old man," Mateo said.

Concho assumed it was Alberto. "He took someone?"

"Cedro."

"Took him where?"

"If I tell you, I'll die." Mateo held up his bloody palm. "But I'm going to die anyway. I'm through with it."

"Where did they go?"

Mateo told him. Concho checked the time. "How long ago?"

"Not long."

Concho stood. "Help will arrive soon."

Mateo coughed out a laugh. Blood dotted his lips. "It's too late."

"Just tell me—you took the girls?"

Mateo nodded. "They paid big money."

"Okay. Help will come soon."

Concho turned and left him. He got back in his truck and turned east.

* * *

CEDRO DROVE SLOWLY. THE OLD TRUCK WOULDN'T GO FAST even if he wanted, but he was in no rush to arrive at the villa where he knew he would die. Bringing an outsider there, especially one with a gun, was suicide. But the old man would kill him too, so until he took a bullet, he wanted to stay alive and hope for a miracle.

Alberto bounced in the passenger seat, the shotgun bobbing up and down between them. They had been driving for about a half hour. They'd moved out of town and up into the hills where things were green and the houses larger and farther apart. Long walls kept prying eyes out of the villas. Parrots cawed from the trees.

Cedro slowed the truck.

"It's here," he said.

Alberto pointed the way. "Keep going."

"You can't just drive up. They'll shoot you."

"You get us in. They know you, right?"

"Yes, but I'm nobody. An errand boy. They won't let me in."

"Try." Alberto gestured with the gun. Cedro turned the truck off the road and started up a steep incline toward a villa on the hill.

* * *

CONCHO TURNED RIGHT AND STEERED HIS TRUCK BETWEEN TWO palm trees planted on either side of the steep driveway. The directions Mateo had given him were good. He knew there was a chance the dying man had lied to him, but he arrived now at the villa that had been described.

Concho had kept his foot down and hadn't slowed. He'd made up time on Alberto and now saw the old man's truck parked ahead of him outside the tall gates to the villa. Concho ground his truck to a halt, not wanting to alert anyone to his presence. He figured there would be cameras all around the property, but maybe not this far down the drive.

He could see Alberto walking up the drive to the gates. He held a shotgun in both hands and out in front of him was a young man walking with his hands up—Alberto's prisoner. Concho ducked into the thick landscaping on the side of the driveway.

Alberto used the butt of the shotgun to bang on the metal gates. He stood back and placed the barrel of the gun in Cedro's back then waited for the gates to open.

Concho questioned whether the man had a plan at all, or if it was just a terrible one.

The gate began to slide open on a track. No one was immediately there waiting, but when the gate reached its full open position, a man eased out from either side, flanking Alberto and Cedro. They each held semiautomatic weapons and began shouting at Alberto in Spanish. Concho couldn't make out what was being said, but the urgency in the voices made it clear.

One of the men fired a burst of shots at the dirt in front of the two men. Alberto dropped the shotgun and lifted his hands high in the air. Concho braced for more shots and to see Alberto crumble in a cloud of blood, but the men stepped out and each took one of the intruders, placed their weapons to the back of the men's skulls, and ushered them inside.

Concho silently cursed to himself as he saw Alberto disappear behind the gates. He knew what he must do. Concho stepped out of the trees and took off at a sprint for the rapidly closing gates.

CHAPTER THIRTY-FOUR

CONCHO SLIPPED BETWEEN THE GATES WITH AN INCH TO SPARE. He moved quickly along the flat metal of the gate and disappeared into the tall trees and bushes inside the compound.

The villa looked like a hotel in Cancún. Lush landscaping and beautifully tiled walkways, fountains and mosaic walls all made a grand entrance to a clay-colored mansion at the top of the small hill. Concho could see the two armed men reach the top of the hill with Alberto and Cedro. They were met by two more men with guns who took them inside.

Concho kept to the edges along the wall that ran the perimeter of the compound. He could reach the side patio without a risk of being seen. In the U-shaped driveway, he saw a Range Rover, a Rolls Royce, a Lamborghini, and an Aston Martin all in a row. A peacock roamed the front lawn by a large fountain.

The two gate guards came back out of the front door, each man slinging the strap of the semi-automatics over their shoulders as they made their way back down the drive to their posts by the gate. Concho watched them go past where he was hidden in the bushes. If he had any hope of getting back out he would have to come this way, so eventually he would meet these men again. He decided to take them out now before they were expecting him.

They had been through the excitement of the day already. At least that's what Concho was hoping they were feeling. Nothing more could drop in unexpectedly, right?

Near the gate was a small hut. Inside were monitors for the many cameras around the property, a mini-fridge, room for two chairs and not much else. Both men went inside.

Concho made a wide circle keeping close to the wall. He came at the hut from the closed side. He could hear two cans being opened. The men celebrating the thwarted attempt to breach the perimeter. He drew both Colts from their holsters and pressed his back against the wall of the hut.

He drew several deep breaths and then spun, ending up facing the open door to the hut, both guns out in front of him.

"Easy, boys."

The two guards froze, cans of beer midway to their mouths.

"Stay still. Easy."

Concho leaned forward and used the barrel of the gun in his left hand to loop under the strap of the machine gun and slip it from the first man's shoulder. He reached over and did the same to the other.

"Kick," he instructed. They both did. Concho holstered one weapon and reached down to pick up the guns. He leaned back out the door and one at a time, he heaved the guns over the wall.

He drew his second gun again and ordered them to, "Walk."

The two men set down their beers and took the same walk they had just forced Alberto to walk, arms up in the same manner.

Concho marched behind them and made them move to where the cars were. He stopped them behind the Rolls Royce.

"Inside," he said. The two men looked confused. "In. In." Concho made gestures with his hands until he was understood.

One of them mimed a key. "*No hay llave.*" No keys.

"Inside," Concho insisted.

One man went to the driver's door and pulled it open. He leaned in and found the trunk release, pressed it, and the trunk opened silently. Concho gave the inside a once-over, looking for weapons of any kind. All he saw was a carpet more plush and luxurious than what was in his house. He pointed them inside.

Both men fit with room to spare inside the Rolls. It had been made for golf clubs and these men were thin and short. Once they were inside, Concho put his finger to his lips to make sure they knew to be quiet, then he shut the lid. It closed almost silently and fit snugly. He knew no matter how much they shouted and kicked, they would be hard to hear outside the car. Fine craftsmanship.

He kept both guns in hand as he went for the front door.

* * *

TITO ALTAMANCA WAS A HEAVY MAN. NOT VERY TALL, BUT HIS belly was large and round. defying any attempts to put a belt around it. He wore suspenders at all times and walked with a waddle. He hadn't always been like that, but years of living the excesses of the man on the ground running operations for The Black Wolf in Mexico had made him slow and soft. He ran things not with any head for business, but based on his name and his relation to The Black Wolf. Tito was his brother-in-law. He'd married Jasmina, The Black Wolf's sister, and from there was made a partner in the business. Jasmina had run off even before The Black Wolf had been arrested. Last word, she was living in Jamaica with the son of a rival drug lord and had undergone such extensive plastic surgery she would be unrecognizable anymore.

Tito let her go. He could have any woman he wanted merely by invoking his power as the proxy leader of the cartel.

He rarely left the compound due to the danger. Theirs was never the largest cartel operation, not even in their region. But by letting the others take the attention of the federales and the DEA in the States, they were allowed to maintain their small operation with little trouble from the authorities. The biggest threats came from other cartels and drug lords who wanted the pests out of the business. So Tito stayed locked away getting fatter and more paranoid, awaiting the day when The Black Wolf would return and the threats would again be focused on him, leaving Tito to make the money and live the lavish life-style, but without the danger.

When his men had awoken him to tell of intruders at the gates, his fear drove him into a state of panic.

Alberto and Cedro were led to the backyard and the stone patio beside the pool. Patio lights up-lit the landscaping and string lights hung above to give the whole area a warm glow. The pool was lit from under the water and it cast a blue shimmer. Tito arrived with a gold-plated pistol in his hand, his robe floating open and his belly protruding out. He wore silk pajama pants and was shirtless, his chest and back coated in tufts of white hair.

"Who the hell are you?"

He moved quickly for a large man. Small, waddling steps driven by fear. He held the gun in his hand and kept it down by his leg.

"Are you the man in charge?" Alberto said.

"Who is this?" Tito asked his subordinates. Nobody had a good answer.

"They showed up at the gate," one man said.

"He had a shotgun," said the other.

"You here to kill me?" Tito said to Alberto. He lifted the gun and waved it toward the two men.

"Did you give the order to take my daughter?" Alberto said.

"Will someone tell me what the hell is going on here?"

Cedro stepped forward. "Don Tito, he came to my house. He is the father of one of the girls who went north to The Black Wolf. He made me bring him here."

"And who the hell are you?"

Cedro seemed confused. "I…Cedro. I work for you."

"And you brought him here, to my door, with a shotgun?" Tito erupted at the accusation. He waved the pistol at Cedro who cowered away.

"He forced me."

"He's an old man."

"He shot Mateo."

"I don't care!"

Tito kept pacing, the robe flapping open around him. His two henchmen stood still, used to this from the boss. Tito stopped in front of Alberto.

"Who sent you here?"

"I came on my own. You stole my daughter from me. And many others."

"You're crazy."

"And you are an evil man."

Tito turned to his men. "Who does he work for?"

"Nobody, Don Tito. As far as we know."

Tito began pacing again. He pointed with the gun at Cedro. "And this one?"

"He works for us."

"Not anymore."

Tito fired. Cedro jerked as a bullet caught him high in the shoulder. He stumbled backward and fell into the pool.

* * *

CONCHO HAD MADE HIS WAY AROUND TO THE BACK OF THE house. He heard loud voices, then a single shot followed by a splash of water. He sped up his movements and was able to see the pool deck. A row of deck chairs were lined along one side, a small waterfall fed a hot tub on the other. A large man in an open robe was pacing in front of Alberto while two armed men flanked him. The skinny man who had come with Alberto was now in the pool, thrashing around.

Concho had no way of knowing how many others were inside. Three he felt he could handle if he kept his element of surprise. But getting Alberto free and making it out of the villa would be two different tasks. Now that the fat man had started shooting, time was running out.

Cedro had made it to the edge of the pool and had flopped halfway out of the water, gasping for breath. He left behind a wide streak of red in the water.

Tito raised the golden gun to Alberto again and shouted something at him Concho couldn't hear. His time to make a plan was over.

Concho took aim at Tito's gun hand. He let the Colt in his left hand fall in the direction of the man to Tito's right. He closed one eye and aimed. He fired but didn't wait to see if his shot had landed. He turned his attention to his left-hand gun and fired at the man standing guard.

Concho moved quickly.

A bullet splintered through Tito's wrist. He dropped the golden gun and screamed out in pain. Alberto dropped to his knees and grabbed the gun from the stone pool deck.

Concho's second shot hit the henchman, but not squarely. He fell back to one of the deck chairs and rolled off onto the stone, drawing his gun as he did.

Stone and palm trees lined the pool deck giving Concho plenty of cover. He fired a shot at the other henchman but missed. He kept moving.

Tito stood on the pool deck screaming and grabbing his wrist. Bright red blood flowed through his fingers and dripped to the stone below.

From behind a large stone Concho took cover and peered out to see what he could see. The two gunmen were crouched low and looking for cover, unsure of who or how many they were dealing with. Concho took aim and fired at the man he'd hit before. This shot put him down and he dropped behind the deck chair. Concho kept moving.

Alberto ran behind the hot tub. The stone gave him shelter there and he fired two shots at the remaining henchman, but missed with both. He had no idea where the shots were coming from all around him, but he knew this was his chance to fight back.

Cedro stumbled forward, sheets of water coming off him as he got himself out of the pool and started running toward the house. The gunman stood from his hiding place and fired, catching Cedro in the chest and dropping the boy in one shot. He hit the stone and bounced back into the water where he floated face down.

As he feared, Concho saw three more men come out of the house, all armed. They all exited from the same door in the back of the house so while they were bunched up, Concho let loose with both guns. He fired four rounds in a tight group and two of the men fell.

Tito began to run toward the hot tub where Alberto was hunkered down. He held a tight grip on his bleeding wrist as he ran and a long, steady scream flowed from his mouth. Alberto stood from behind the hot tub and aimed the golden gun at its former owner. He fired three shots and Tito was hit three times. He crumbled and fell to his knees. He bounced on his protruding belly and it spun him off to the right where he rolled like a bowling ball toward the water. He splashed and bobbed several times as his weight tried to pull him to the bottom.

Alberto had been exposed and the remaining men took aim. Shots came fast and the old man barely had time to duck back behind the stone of the hot tub.

Concho saw a path forward, but it was a risk. The volley of bullets coming at Alberto meant he didn't have much time. Concho stood from his hiding place and ran toward the pool. With the men distracted by Alberto's position, Concho could move freely. He ran to the edge of the pool and leaped. He landed on the diving board, barely reaching with his long stride. In one continuous move he used the spring of the board to launch him across to the far side of the pool. While he was in the air, Concho began to fire.

The first man who had been out there since the start caught a bullet in his neck and went down. The new man turned to see where the shots were coming from. He saw a six foot four Indian flying through the air and his mouth gaped open. Concho fired once and hit him in the forehead.

He landed on the stone, now wet with splashed pool water and blood. He stayed low and checked for any movement.

"Alberto?" he called out.

The old man's head peered up over the edge of the hot tub stone.

"Are you hit?"

"No," Alberto answered.

"Are there more inside?"

"I'm not sure."

"Follow me."

Concho stood and heard a short groan. He aimed down at one of the men he'd hit coming out of the house and fired a kill shot. He paused to reload both Colts. Each one had been fully discharged. One more pull of the trigger would have fallen on an empty chamber.

Alberto joined him.

"I must thank you again, it seems."

"Wait until we make it out of here."

Alberto dropped the golden gun into the pool and picked up one of the fallen semi-automatics.

"You lead."

CHAPTER THIRTY-FIVE

THE INSIDE OF THE VILLA WAS CHILLY. CONCHO LED THE WAY through a high-ceilinged living room that felt more like a hotel lobby than a residence. They moved past an L-shaped leather sofa and toward a hallway that led to the front door.

Concho heard feet on the tile floor. He motioned to Alberto to get flat against the wall. Two women in traditional housekeeper uniforms came scurrying from the kitchen. They were scared, having heard the gunfire, and were headed for the door. The woman in front saw Concho and his drawn gun and let out a small shriek. The woman behind her cowered and lifted her hands in the air.

"It's okay," Concho said. "It's okay. All over now."

The woman in front stood suddenly and her arm flicked out. A small knife shot from her hand toward Alberto. He yelped as it landed in his thigh. The women ran for the door. Concho sighted down on them, but held off taking a shot. They both cried out and prayed out loud as they ran.

Alberto dropped his gun and slumped to the floor. Concho went to him.

"Are you okay?"

Alberto nodded and grit his teeth against the pain. Concho

reached down and put a hand on the handle of the small paring knife.

"Hang on." He yanked up in one swift movement. Alberto cried out as the knife came free. It had been about an inch and a half embedded in his leg. Concho let the knife fall to the floor. He got up and went back to the living room. He went to one of the heavy velvet curtains and untied the thick sash there. He brought it back to Alberto and tied it around his leg as tight as he could. He brought up the knife and cut away the excess. Alberto's pant leg was already soaked in blood.

"Can you walk?"

"I think so."

Concho helped the old man up and held his arm as he tried for a single step. His leg collapsed under him.

"Hold on," Concho said. He bent and picked up Alberto onto his shoulders in a fireman's carry. It would hinder his ability to use a weapon if they ran into any more gunmen, but the urgency to get Alberto out and to a hospital made it the right decision.

The two housekeepers had left the front door open and Concho carried Alberto through.

They passed by the Rolls Royce but heard nothing. He would have to tell the federales of the two men inside when he reported what had happened here. Concho carried Alberto out to his truck and left the old man's rusty pickup behind.

"I will take care of this," Alberto said.

"No offense, but you haven't been doing a great job so far."

"I mean I will clean this up. Many men in the village will help. They will be glad to carry away the dead bodies of the men who are taking our children."

"Thanks for the offer, but I need to go the official route on this one. I need the computers, the files, any info inside. I need a direct link to The Black Wolf."

"Do you not have it?"

"I have it enough for myself, I need it airtight for US prosecutors. But look, the most important thing is that we cut off the head of the snake, right? No more daughters are going missing."

Alberto put a hand on Concho's arm. "Thank you."

"Hey, when you get back, you tell them whatever you want to. Be the big hero. Whatever you do, don't mention that a woman knifed you in the leg."

"That secret dies with me," Alberto said.

* * *

ALBERTO DIRECTED HIM TO A HOSPITAL. THEY TOOK THE OLD man in a wheelchair and brought him to get his leg stitched up.

Concho got on the phone to the federales and told them the story. He left Alberto in the care of the doctors and went back to the villa to meet them.

Six cars worth of federales arrived and they swept the property looking for any more gunmen but found none. Concho was questioned, made to show his ranger badge, and then sat down with a guard to await further questioning.

Night turned to morning and he called north to Shaw while he waited and filled in the boss on what went down.

"Jesus, Ten-Wolves. Made a hell of a mess, didn't you?"

"I made a direct connection to The Black Wolf is what I did."

"How?"

"Once they're done searching this place, I'm sure they'll find enough evidence to link this operation with him up there at Bigfoot. At the least, no more girls will be coming out of this area."

"Well, that's something."

"There is one more already in the States. She was taken three days ago."

"Any idea where? There's been no activity at the house we busted."

"No idea. But we know where she's going. I say we go clean

house at Bigfoot and bust that warden and all the guards on the take."

"Okay. I'll start that in motion. You get your ass back here and try not to kill anyone else on your way, got it?"

"I'll do my best."

"Do better than that, Concho."

"I make no promises."

* * *

CONCHO WENT BY THE HOSPITAL ON HIS WAY OUT. ALBERTO WAS recovering in a room, a large ball of white gauze wrapped around his leg.

"That was foolish, what you did," Concho said.

"I let the anger get the best of me," Alberto said.

"It's your daughter, I understand, but still…"

"Thank you for coming to save me. I already owed you, but now…"

Concho waved him away. "You can thank me by staying out of trouble. And tell the police everything you know. Get people in your town to do the same. The men are gone now. There is no threat to the people anymore."

Alberto scoffed. "You know how it is with rats. You kill one, and ten more come out from behind the wall."

"Well, we're going to cut off the head of the rat king. No more Black Wolf."

"You really think you can stop him for good?"

"It's my job."

Concho tapped the badge pinned to his shirt pocket.

CHAPTER THIRTY-SIX

WORD TRAVELED FAST FROM DOWN SOUTH. SOMEONE MADE A phone call, someone sent a text, and next thing he knew, James Lee Morris's phone was ringing with an international call.

"Yeah?" he answered.

He got the full rundown. How many dead, the federales crawling all over. Suddenly brave, now that the men were dead and they had a Texas Ranger to thank for it.

"What a mess," he said.

"What do we do now?" the voice on the line said.

"Get to the place in Sabinas. Wait for word there. The Black Wolf is coming home."

He ended the call and checked his watch. James Lee made a decision. He'd move up the timeline even more, get The Black Wolf out of prison and across the border. Then he was done. He knew The Black Wolf would reward him. It would be enough to get out, get to the islands. He could feel the noose tightening and he wanted his neck free.

* * *

James Lee never waited long in the visitor's area for The Black Wolf to arrive. It wasn't like in the old days. Cash money never changed hands. Of course, there was a time when all it would take would be a fifty-dollar bill folded in the palm when he shook hands with a guard who needed a little extra that week. Now the payoffs came in hundreds, all transferred directly into Zelle or PayPal accounts.

The Black Wolf entered the visitor's area. They were the only two in the gray room and the guard who had escorted him downstairs left them to it.

James Lee filled the boss in on the troubles in Mexico.

"So, the long and short of it is that you need to be ready to move in the next twenty-four to forty-eight hours."

"James Lee, I've been ready to go since the day I got here," The Black Wolf said.

"Well, we're only gonna get one shot at this, so on the off chance you found God while you were in here, I'd pray if have a mind to."

"I trust you."

"With this ranger out there screwing us at every turn, I wish I trusted the whole process right on down the line, but it'll have to do."

The Black Wolf drummed his knuckles on the metal table, nervous energy escaping through his fingers. A small smile reached his lips. James Lee wasn't sure he'd ever seen him smile other than one that was meant to intimidate.

"I'll be ready."

The Black Wolf stood and walked out. James Lee started down the hall for the exit, his mind a blur of all the people he needed to contact and make sure things were in place. He almost bumped into Warden Scalise.

Scalise tried to give him a tough stare-down. "You know we typically frown on too many visits so close together. Kinda makes us nervous about what is being discussed, you know?"

Now it was James Lee's turn to try an intimidating smile.

"Warden, we gave you a chance to make a little extra on the side," James Lee said. "You turned us down. When you did, you also gave up any right to tell me what to do or who to visit or how many times. And as for what we discuss? That ain't none of your goddamn business."

"If you or that certain inmate intend to cause any disruption to my institution, you're damn right it's my business."

"A little late for that, Warden."

James Lee pushed past Scalise, shoving aside his shoulder with his own. The warden stumbled to the side as he passed.

"I'm serious, Morris. I give your guy plenty of latitude here, but if he disturbs the peace at all, that agreement is over."

James Lee stopped and turned back to face the warden. "You ever show this side of you to the wife? I bet she'd be impressed that you still had a spine. Might be the only thing on your body that's still capable of getting stiff."

"You leave my damn wife out of it."

"Don't act like you don't know how the game works, warden. If I were you, I'd stop talking in case you say something you can't take back. Go back to your office, draw the blinds, and look the other way. It's what you're best at."

James Lee turned on his heel and walked out. Near the final gate, he spotted Roy and changed his trajectory to approach the guard.

"Mr. Morris," Roy said, a mixture of respect and fear.

James Lee grabbed him by the shirt and pushed him up against the chain-link fence. James Lee got close to Roy's face and spoke low.

"Get your house in order, you hear me? We're making the move. If you want to see a dime out of this, you make sure it runs like clockwork. And keep a lid on that goddamn warden of yours."

"Y-yes, Mr. Morris. I'll handle it. A hundred percent."

"If this goes the wrong way, there will be scorched earth

like you have never seen before, you understand me? You have no idea the reach of these people if they want to right a wrong. Four horsemen of the apocalypse will ride into town and there won't be nothing you can do about it."

"I get it. I understand."

James Lee let Roy go. "You damn well better."

CHAPTER THIRTY-SEVEN

CONCHO STOPPED AT A WAFFLE HOUSE ON THE TEXAS SIDE OF the border and had a plate of eggs and sausage with hash browns scattered, smothered, and covered. Before he went inside, he dug out a slightly bent paperback from the glove compartment of his truck. It was one of the Hard Case Crime line of vintage reissues and he bought it because of the title—SAY IT WITH BULLETS. So far it has lived up to the lurid title and cover art.

He tried not to dwell on the irony of his relaxation after such an intense encounter as the one he'd had in Mexico being reading about murder. He hadn't realized how ravenous he was as he held the book splayed open with his left hand and forked food into his mouth with his right in a constant motion. When he finished, he thought about getting a waffle too, but he thought better of it. He paid up and got back in his truck and drove straight to the mall.

The food in his stomach and the events of the past twenty-four hours made Concho sleepy and he debated bypassing the mall and going home, but he wanted to see Maria. He parked and walked to her office.

He knocked, and she said, "Come in."

When she looked up and saw him, Maria stood like she'd been bit on the behind by a rattlesnake. She dodged around the corner of her desk and wrapped him in a hug.

"When did you get back?"

"Just now," he said. "I haven't even been home yet."

She pulled back and gave him a sly look. "Ahh, couldn't stay away from me, huh?"

"I knew you'd want to know how it went. I figured you might be worried about me."

She waved the idea away. "About you? Not my big, strong man." Maria leaned forward and kissed him.

When they broke, he said, "It went well, by the way."

"Good. So you're home for good now?"

"One more trip up north," he said.

Maria slapped his chest.

"But it'll take me a day or two to set it up with Shaw and to coordinate with the cops up there. We might need to bring DEA or the prison system into it, too."

"So I get you for at least a day?" she said. "How generous."

"Why don't you let me show you how generous I can be," Concho said. He reached behind him and locked the door.

"I won't say no to that," Maria said.

* * *

"She don't look good, bro."

Hugo and Mateo stood over the girl who was laid out on the bathroom floor. Her eyes fluttered open, then closed again. Her skin was pale and milky. Bones showed through on her shoulders and her ribs.

"She needs food or something," Hugo said.

"It's like having a damn dog for a pet," Rubén said.

"I'll go get her something."

"Get some medicine too. Maybe she's sick."

Hugo bent down to look at her more closely. "What do you think she needs?"

Rubén shrugged and turned away. "Hell if I know, bro."

Hugo stood quickly, recoiling. "Damn, man, she's bleeding."

Rubén turned back around and came to stand over Hugo's shoulder. They both looked down at her and they saw the blood between her legs. She had soaked through her underwear and leaked blood onto the white tile floor.

"Damn, bro."

"What the hell happened to her?"

"I dunno, bro."

The girl, Consuela, opened her eyes and rolled onto her back. "Idiots," she said.

Hugo and Rubén watched her carefully, but didn't speak.

"I need tampons," she said. When they gave her only a blank stare back, she said, "For...you know."

Understanding hit Hugo and he took a step back. "You do?"

She gestured to her bloody clothing. "Yeah." Consuela held her head, fighting a wave of headache and a bit of nausea. "And he's right, I need food. A burger. Something with iron. I get low iron when..."

"Okay, okay."

"And get some pills for a migraine."

Hugo slapped Rubén's shoulder. "Write this down."

Consuela put a hand over her eyes. "And turn off the light, will you?"

Hugo clicked the switch and they both stepped back into the hotel room.

"You gonna go get that stuff?" Hugo said.

"I guess. Where do I go?"

"Grocery store, I guess."

"That's embarrassing, bro. I don't wanna buy that mess."

"You wanna clean up blood all over the place?"

Rubén recoiled and made a sour face. They'd both been around plenty of blood before. Something about this made it different.

Hugo shrugged. "Just say they're for your sister."

Rubén slapped the wall with an open palm. "I wish they'd just make the call and we can get her out of here."

"Yeah, well, until they do, she's our responsibility. You wanna deliver this mess to *El Lobo Negro?*"

Rubén huffed out a blast of air. "Fine, bro." He snatched up the keys to the car on his way out the door and made a point to slam it loud.

Hugo went and sat on the bed, trying to keep his distance from Consuela and her issue. Hugo's phone rang. He thought about what an idiot Rubén was if he couldn't make it ten seconds without calling for help. They were just tampons. He checked the face of his phone and saw it was James Lee calling.

"Hello?"

With no preamble, James Lee said, "Change of plans."

Damn it, Hugo thought. "Oh, yeah?"

"We're canceling delivery. We don't need her anymore."

"Huh?"

Hugo could tell James Lee was annoyed at having to repeat himself. "Don't bring her up here. Get rid of her."

"Get rid of her?"

"Yeah. Are you stupid, kid, or just deaf?"

"Get rid of her how?"

James Lee's voice rose in volume and pitch. "I don't care. Just don't bring her here and I don't want to read about her on the news. Just get rid of her, *entender?*"

Hugo knew better than to make James Lee mad. Even if he didn't fully understand, he knew he needed to fake it. "Yeah, yeah, no problem. We got it."

"Good. Take care of it." He hung up with no goodbye.

Hugo slowly took the phone down from his face and stared at the girl on the bathroom floor.

"Can I get a cup of water?" she asked.

"Yeah, sure." Hugo unwrapped one of the plastic-covered cups and ran the bathroom sink faucet until it turned cold. He handed the cup to Consuela. She drank the cup in three long gulps.

"God, my head is splitting."

Hugo refilled the cup and handed it back to her, seeing her differently now. For all the others his job had only been to deliver them. They'd be in the back seat or sometimes the trunk of his car for a few hours, then he'd never see them again. He never knew their names. Never knew they got headaches or had to think about the fact that they had a menstrual cycle.

And he'd certainly never had to kill one before.

CHAPTER THIRTY-EIGHT

CONCHO KISSED MARIA WHILE STANDING IN THE DOORWAY TO her office. After the hour he'd spent with her, he was more exhausted than ever.

"Go home and get some rest," she said. "You're gonna need it for when I get home."

He smiled and then kissed her again. "I'll be sure to hydrate."

He got back to his truck and wasn't sure he could even make the drive home. When he did arrive back at the house, he called Shaw to check in.

"I'm expecting a report from the federales," Shaw said. "It'll be at least a day."

"It feels weird to bust a guy who's already been busted."

"Yeah, but this time they can lock him in solitary and cut him off from all his contacts in the cartel. And if there are guards helping him for payoffs—"

Concho cut in. "Oh, there are."

"—then we can take them down too. Maybe they'll see a little time behind bars themselves."

Shaw was sharing his intel with the DEA, the prison authorities and the local police around Bigfoot. Concho knew any time that many agencies needed to coordinate, it meant a bureaucratic nightmare and miles of red tape.

"Never easy, this job," Shaw said.

"No. You said that right."

"Okay, Ten-Wolves. Good work. Check in with me tomorrow and we'll see what we've heard."

"Okay, boss. Thanks."

Concho downed a large glass of ice water and fell into bed.

* * *

RUBÉN RETURNED WITH A WHITE PLASTIC BAG, CLUTCHING IT TO his chest as if he were carrying a pound of heroin.

"I got it." He dropped the bag on the bed, eager to get rid of it. Hugo opened the bag and took out a box of tampons and a bottle of migraine pills. He gave them a quick glance but didn't know what he was checking for, then tossed them into the bathroom.

"Here, try these."

Consuela opened her eyes and dragged herself up to sit with her back against the tub. She lifted the box of tampons and the pill bottle. "It'll have to do. Don't suppose you got me a new pair of underwear, did you?"

Rubén's eyes went wide. "Nobody told me to!"

"Great," she said. Consuela went to close the door.

Hugo shouted, "Not all the way."

She left the door open a crack. When she was safely hidden behind the door, Hugo went to Rubén and spoke low.

"We got an issue."

"Yeah?" Rubén said. "What is it?"

"James Lee called. They don't want her no more. Said to get rid of her."

Rubén studied Hugo's face looking for some indication this was a joke. "Get rid of her, like…get *rid* of her?"

Hugo nodded. "Yeah."

"Damn, bro."

"That's what I'm saying."

They both stood and thought about the implications. Neither one had ever killed anyone before. Rubén hadn't even been in the room when someone else did it, though Hugo had. This was a different level.

"How do we...what do we do?" Rubén asked. They had no guns. Hugo had a knife, but none of the girls ever gave them enough trouble to need a gun. Most came to them drugged out, and they only had them along on a ride north, not long enough to need self-defense.

"I don't know, dude," Hugo said.

"Damn, bro," Rubén said again. "That's cold."

"That's James Lee, man. You know that dude."

Rubén sat down on the bed. "Do we do it here?"

"No, man. He said she can't be found. She's gotta disappear."

"Like out in the desert?"

"Yeah. That's a good idea."

Hearing he had a good idea on how to kill a girl made Rubén's stomach rumble. He didn't want to become a killer. Especially not a killer of women.

"Hey," Ruben said. "They just said get rid of her, right?"

"That's what he said."

"Seems a shame to just kill her and dump her body somewhere, right?"

Hugo thought of it, and looked at the bathroom door. "Yeah."

"So what if we get rid of her some other way."

Hugo folded his arms across his chest, intrigued. "How?"

The bathroom door swung open. Consuela was standing now, her long T-shirt hung low over her hips, covering her. She held her underwear dangling off one finger of her right hand. It had a dark stain covering most of it.

"Yeah, I'm gonna need a new pair."

When she was first taken, Consuela figured she'd be dead by now. The other girls had vanished and never come home.

Then they heard word that Ximena had been rescued. A day and a half later, Consuela was in the back of a van headed for the border.

When Hugo and Rubén first brought her to the motel, she figured she was going to be raped by both of them, but they had been respectable. As respectable as kidnappers could be, she figured. They weren't the final stop for her, she knew. Something else waited at the end of the line. She focused her fear on surviving the next five minutes, then the next five after that. She blocked out the next steps for her and focused on the moment. So far it had kept her fear tamped down, then the migraine came along to distract her further. And the more time she spent with these two, the more she figured they were morons who were harmless.

She dropped the underwear into the sink and ran warm water over them, trying to rinse out the stains. She cupped her hands and took in a mouthful of water, then swallowed a migraine pill.

Hugo said to her, "Can you give us a minute to talk?"

She looked around the small bathroom like *where the hell am I going to go?* Then she silently closed the door, leaving a crack open.

Hugo whispered to Rubén, "Okay, how do we get rid of her then?"

"So we were taking her to some men, right?"

"The Black Wolf."

"Among others. So she's desirable. She's got a value. So why don't we sell her to someone else?"

"What the hell are you talking about?"

"I mean, we find someone willing to buy her. He takes her away. We got rid of her. Problem solved."

Hugo thought it over. He wanted to hate the idea, but he didn't.

"How do we do that?"

"The casino?"

Hugo thought *that* over. It made sense to him. There would

be men there who might be in the market for a girl. Mostly, Hugo was eager for any excuse not to kill her.

"Let's try it."

"Hell, yeah." Rubén reached out and shook Hugo's hand.

"But you have to go get her new underwear now."

The smile dropped off Rubén's face.

CHAPTER THIRTY-NINE

ROY CLIMBED THE STEPS TO THE SECOND FLOOR OF CELLS, HIS feet clanking on the metal stairs like broken cymbals. He walked slowly, deliberately, with a glazed look on his face. When he reached the top, he turned to face The Black Wolf's open cell door. The notorious inmate was sitting with his feet up and watching a soccer match on the flat-screen TV in his cell. Two other men were with him, each sitting on a bunk bolted to the wall. Roy stood in the doorway.

The Black Wolf looked up and noticed him, finally.

"I just heard," Roy said.

The Black Wolf looked confused. "Heard what?"

"My wife is dead."

On the TV, the crowd roared at a missed goal. The Black Wolf almost said, "Ah!" as he connected the pieces about Roy and his tattle-tale ex-wife, but instead merely nodded.

"Ex-wife," he said. "And you said she was a bitch."

"So you did it?" Roy stood, almost catatonic. The shock still fresh with him.

"She had a big mouth."

"You did it."

The Black Wolf set his feet down on the concrete floor.

One of his henchmen muted the TV. All around them, the noises of the cell block continued on.

"She talked to that ranger. You came and told me. What else was I supposed to do?"

"But…you're leaving. James Lee has us jumping through hoops to get this set up. You'll be gone from here in no time. You couldn't wait a few days? You had to kill her?"

"Amigo, I don't tell you how to do your job." He snapped his fingers and the henchman on the top bunk hopped down and took a thin cigar from his pocket. He handed it to The Black Wolf and lit a gold lighter. The Black Wolf held the cigar to the flame, never breaking eye contact with Roy, and puffed until he got the smoke going.

"You got anything else to say, Roy?" he asked.

"I can't wait until you're gone. I was wrong to take money from you. You got no loyalty. You got no morals. You need Jesus in your life. That's the only thing that'll help you."

All three men in the cell burst out laughing. The Black Wolf clenched the cigar in his mouth and puffed smoke with each guffaw.

"Has he helped you, Jesus? Divorced. Working this crappy job. Taking money on the side from me. Living in a dust bowl. How has he helped you?"

"All she did was run her mouth a little bit. She didn't have to die for it."

The Black Wolf changed his demeanor in an instant. He hurled the cigar to the floor. "You hated her! She kicked you out. She didn't love you."

Roy was near tears. Hearing of June's death had dredged up all the hurt and broken-hearted memories of the divorce. Roy hadn't dated anyone seriously since she kicked him out. He put up a tough front when he saw her or when he had to deal with her lawyer, but truth was, he would've taken her back in a second if she'd ever asked.

"Y'know what?" Roy said. "You're on your own. I'm not

helping you bust out of here. James Lee can kiss my ass, and so can you."

He stood his ground, spreading his shoulders to fill the open space of the doorway where the cell door bars should have been closed.

"You don't need me," The Black Wolf said. "Then I don't need you." He motioned with his hand. A small, simple gesture that the two men behind him understood immediately. With a slight flick of his wrist, he had ordered a man killed.

The two men stepped forward, one on either side of The Black Wolf's chair. The Black Wolf didn't need his TV or his soccer match anymore. He had a new entertainment to focus on.

Roy shrank from his puffed-up stance. He knew what was coming. He felt foolish for trying to take on the big boss. But he was still a guard, still had some authority.

"Stay right where you are," he said.

The two men ignored him and kept on advancing slowly.

Roy drew his taser. Handheld, the size of a TV remote. It didn't have the full power of what the cops on the outside carried, but it would put a man down. Two might be difficult. He held the taser in his right hand and set his feet apart, ready for an attack. The two men raised their fists. They had both spent years in the gym lifting weights here at Bigfoot. Their deep tanned skin was etched with blue ink tattoos, some from the outside and many from inside. Very little artistry. Each man had a full moon with a silhouette of a black wolf howling in the center of it on their bicep.

The man to his left moved first. Roy swung the taser and pressed the button. It caught the man's forearm as he swung at Roy. The arcs of electricity touched skin for only a second. The man yelped and recoiled his arm, but he didn't get a full blast enough to go down. The man on Roy's right lunged forward.

Roy backhanded him across his cheek, missing him entirely with the taser, but stunning him enough that no fist landed on Roy. With attacks from both sides, Roy had to split his attention. He pushed out with the taser toward the man on his left again, keeping the button down, the sparks clicking in the air between the two metal prongs. He'd run out of charge before too long, but he only could worry about the next few seconds.

The man dodged the taser and ducked low. The Black Wolf watched with a smile on his face. This was great entertainment.

Across the cell block, other men began to notice the fight. They started cheering and banging on the bars of their cells like caged animals.

The man to his right landed a punch to Roy's gut. He bent and puffed out air. The other man stayed bent low and rammed forward, driving Roy out of the doorway and only to the metal grating of the landing to the second floor. A cheer went up from the cellblock louder than the crowd at the soccer match.

Two guards on the downstairs floor perked up. When they looked and saw what cell the commotion came from, they hesitated.

The man on Roy's right dove for the fallen taser. Roy struggled to catch his wind as he felt the metal grating dig into his back. He looked up and the taser crackled with blue sparks only inches from his face. He tried to scurry backward toward the steps. The taser came down and pressed firmly into his neck. The world went bright white for a flash and then black.

Roy convulsed and then, when the taser was removed from his neck, went still. The man with the taser stood straight, holding the weapon in his palm, happy about his new toy. Both men looked back to The Black Wolf who gave the slightest nod.

Another roar from the crowd of inmate onlookers as each man grabbed an arm and a leg and lifted Roy from the deck. A rhythmic chant and percussive banging began as the men pounded on their cell bars in a tribal beat.

The two men lifted Roy to their shoulders and he came to, squirming suddenly against his attackers. The black wolf tattoo on both men writhed and pulsated on their muscles. They paused to take in the chant and the beat. The whole building pulsed with it. The bars rattled, the floor rocked, the concrete echoed.

The pace of the pounding sped up, reaching a frenzied speed. Roy shouted for them to stop and put him down. The men hoisted Roy over their heads and launched him over the railing. He fell, head first, toward the floor below. The men all howled in primal release.

Roy hit the concrete floor with the top of his skull. The sound penetrated even the cacophonous howls and beating of bars. A stain of red spread out from his cracked skull as the rest of his body hit in a limp pile.

Cheers rose up, a celebration and a blood lust.

The Black Wolf sat in his chair and clapped.

"At least now they will be together," he said, but no one heard him over the din.

CHAPTER FORTY

HUGO DROVE THE CAR INTO THE PARKING LOT OF THE LUCKY Eagle Casino and Hotel on the Kickapoo Reservation just a few miles from Eagle Pass. The wide lot of black tarmac spread out in all directions from the casino building. Plenty of parking if the entire town of Eagle Pass decided to try their luck all at once. About seventy percent of the spots were open in the middle of the day. Hugo parked in a completely empty row far from the entrance.

"Why are you parking all the way back here?" Rubén asked.

"We're trying not to draw attention," Hugo said.

Consuela was in the back seat with Rubén, her wrists and ankles tied and covered with a towel they stole from the motel. The rope dug into her skin and rubbed it raw. She wore the new clothes Rubén had bought for her and the shapeless athletic shorts were made even less flattering by being a full size too big. The underwear she had on underneath were two sizes too large.

"Okay," Hugo said. "You stay here. I'll go see if I can find a buyer." He unbuckled his seatbelt and moved to get out.

"Why do you get to go?" Rubén asked.

"Someone has to stay here."

"Yeah, but why me?"

"Do you know anyone who wants to buy a girl?"

"Well...no."

"There you go." Hugo got out. He left the keys in and the car so the air conditioner could run. The blacktop heated up the bottom of his shoes as soon as he stepped onto it.

"Wait," Rubén said. "Do you know someone?"

"No." Hugo slammed the door and started walking toward the casino entrance.

Consuela didn't like that phrase *buy a girl*. What did that mean? They were trying to sell her? To who? She moved her hands and her feet, but it only rubbed her skin more raw under the ropes.

"Hey, can you loosen these ropes?" she said. "It really hurts."

"Yeah, so you can run away? I don't think so."

Her initial fear had calcified into a dull worry and a wary eye kept on a way out and away from these two.

* * *

HUGO FELT THE BLAST OF COLD AIR ONCE HE WAS INSIDE. THE casino floor was loud with electronic noises from the slot machines. The carpet had swirling lines like a maze that led nowhere and the lighting was like midfield at a Cowboys game. He scanned around trying to decide if the gaming tables were a better bet, or the bar. He settled on the circular bar in the middle of the floor. Men at the tables would be distracted by the games. Men at the bar were either busted broke or flush with cash and looking to spend it.

He did think maybe they should have waited until night when there were more people, but they wanted to be rid of her as quickly as possible. The easy way would be to drive out into the big empty and kill her, like James Lee wanted. But to Hugo, there was nothing easy about that.

The noise was a little dampened inside the bar, but the gap was filled with competing TVs showing baseball on one, a soccer match on another and a rerun of the NBA Finals with Michael Jordan and the Bulls on another.

There were three men at the bar. The one on the far end looked about to pass out into his drink. Must have lost his shirt at the tables. Hugo ignored him. A second man wore a suit, but his jacket was off and draped over the seat next to him where Hugo could see a drink glass there with a lipstick stain on the rim. Waiting for his wife to come back and join him. Probably not in the girl-buying mood.

The third man was alone. He wore an ivory-colored western shirt with pearl buttons and black stitching, a cowboy hat over his long, straight hair and snakeskin boots. Hugo figured him for one of the tribe.

Hugo sat down in the seat next to him.

The bartender was bent down changing a keg, and didn't notice Hugo arrive.

"By yourself?" Hugo asked.

The man in the hat turned to him. "Huh?"

"I said, you by yourself?"

"Yep."

He lifted his beer bottle and took a sip.

"That's a shame."

The man turned back to Hugo, studying him. "Why?"

"Man shouldn't be alone. He needs companionship. He needs a woman by his side."

The man rolled his eyes thinking, *great, a pimp.*

"I don't need to pay for my girls by the hour, okay friend," the man said. "I want companionship, I can make a call, okay? I got plenty of girls when I need them."

"Oh, I'm sure you do, I'm sure you do. I'm not talking about by the hour, though."

The man set down his beer and pushed his hat off his forehead to get a good long look at Hugo. "You're not some kind of a pimp?"

"Me? No."

"Well, you oughta record yourself and listen back to it because you sure as hell sound like some kind of a pimp."

Hugo reached out and pulled a bowl of shelled peanuts close to him. He put three in his mouth. "Oh, I'm selling something. But it's more of a final sale sort of thing. Not a rental."

"Mister, if you got something to say, come out and say it." He nodded toward the TV over the bar. "The Astros are getting killed and my mood ain't the best."

Hugo flipped a peanut off his thumb and tried to catch it in mid-air. It bounced off his chin.

"How would you like a companion that's all yours, all the time? Do whatever you like, whenever you like."

The man looked intrigued now. "What?"

"A woman. Very attractive. She is looking for companionship too. For one payment, she is all yours. Keep her as long as you like?"

The man rotated his body on the stool, his attention off the game now. "What are you saying, friend?"

"I have a woman. For the right price, she can be yours."

"So you are a pimp."

"No. I'm a salesman."

He held up his finger, trying to understand. "So not for an hour, not for the night. I get to keep her?"

"For a price."

"How much?"

Crap. He and Rubén hadn't discussed price. So far, he'd gotten farther along than he expected. It was all going much smoother and much faster than he anticipated. He studied the man, trying to find the right number not to scare him off, but not too low that he and Rubén wouldn't benefit from it.

"Ten thousand."

Hugo waited, his throat dry, for the response. The man thought about it, blank-faced, impossible to read.

"Cash?"

Hugo hadn't thought about that either, but it seemed like

the best way.

"Yeah, cash."

"You got a picture?" the man asked. "She around?" He looked across the bar.

"You bring me the cash and I bring you the girl."

"I don't have it on me."

"By the time you come back, I'll have the girl here for you."

The man looked Hugo up and down. He ended on his eyes which he held for a long time. "Okay," he said. "Gimme fifteen minutes."

Hugo almost yelped. He'd done it. He tried to hide his giddy excitement. He didn't have to kill the girl and he was going to get ten grand.

He thought about the handoff. In the bar was not a good place to bring a girl bound at the wrists and ankles.

"Meet around back," he said.

The man paused mid-slide off his seat. "Around back?"

"You don't want to do this in plain sight, do you?"

The man surveyed the bar and the casino floor, the cameras in the ceiling. "No, I guess not. Okay. Around back, fifteen minutes."

"I'll be there."

The man fit the cowboy hat back firmly on his head and walked out. The bartender finally stood up and noticed Hugo.

"What can I get you?" he said.

"Nothing," Hugo said and rushed out of the room.

* * *

THE MAN IN THE PEARL-BUTTON SHIRT WATCHED HUGO WALK out the front door. He pulled a cell phone from his pocket and dialed.

Concho Ten-Wolves answered, sleep in his voice. "Yeah?"

"Concho? It's Bernie Twin-Moons. I have a situation down here at the Lucky Eagle."

CHAPTER FORTY-ONE

CONCHO CUPPED WATER IN HIS TWO HANDS, THREW IT AT HIS face and slapped himself awake. He'd made Bernie repeat himself three times to make sure he wasn't dreaming the call. Someone at the Lucky Eagle was trying to sell Bernie a woman.

Bernie was a drinker, that was no secret. Not the worst on the Rez by any stretch, but everyone knew where to find him if you went looking. A bar, a liquor store, any place with a cold beer and a chair. The Lucky Eagle had been a favorite of Bernie's since it opened. Always open, always crowded, always exciting. This, though, was a new one even for him.

After Bernie had reassured Concho he hadn't had more than two beers, Concho told him to sit tight and keep the guy there.

He was in a hurry, so he left the twin Double Eagles behind and took his Smith & Wesson .38 with the two-inch barrel. Easier to conceal.

He got in his truck and ignored the speed limit. If anyone tried to pull him over, he'd invite them with him to bust a human trafficker.

Bernie had to be wrong. There had to be some sort of

misunderstanding. A language barrier, maybe. He'd said the guy was Mexican. But if there was even a slight chance that this was the other missing girl from down south, that he could return another daughter to her family, then he needed to take the old drunk seriously.

He wasn't so confident that he called for backup, though. He didn't want to have a cadre of squad cars, lights and sirens running, descend on the Lucky Eagle only to have it turn out to be a false alarm. He'd have to endure a lot of jokes from the other Rangers about Bernie's love of "fire water" and Concho's trusting nature. In reality, Concho thought he was pretty good at sniffing out a lie.

Already the looming hotel tower was in sight. Concho hoped like hell Bernie was wrong about this for the girl's sake, but he also hoped he was right for his own.

* * *

BERNIE CHECKED HIS WATCH. FOURTEEN MINUTES HAD PASSED already. No sign of Concho Ten-Wolves. And no sign of ten thousand dollars in cash. That wasn't going to happen unless he walked onto the floor and robbed the blackjack table.

He stood near the rear door of the casino floor, by the employee entrance to the kitchens. The noise was steady and the lights bright in every corner. He'd have to stall the guy, keep him occupied until Concho got there. But if he was going to do that, he needed another beer.

* * *

"THE FIRST ONE?"

"First one." Hugo beamed proudly. He checked the time on his cell phone. "Let's get moving." He opened the rear door where Consuela sat. She cowered away from him. Rubén had already untied her, making her presentable to the buyer.

"Why don't we drive over?" Rubén asked.

"Because they got cameras and stuff back there, man. That's where the armored cars do their stuff."

"Then they're gonna see us anyway."

"No, man, keep your back to the cameras. Just face away from the building. But this way they don't see the license plate." He tapped his forehead to indicate how smart he had been to think this all through.

Rubén had no counter-argument so he shrugged and got out on his side. Hugo reached in for Consuela. She kicked out and caught him on the chin with her bare heel. She hadn't been wearing shoes when she was taken in Mexico, and they hadn't gotten her new ones.

Hugo cursed loudly and fell backward out the door onto the hot asphalt.

Consuela lunged forward and stepped on him as she bolted away from the car.

Rubén watched it all from the other side of the car. She ran quickly away.

"Damn it!" Rubén started after her at a sprint.

* * *

Bernie waited until the bartender turned away and then took his beer bottle and left the bar. A policy violation, but not one they enforced too strictly. After all, the minute you sat down at a table, you could get any drink you wanted. It made sure the cocktail waitresses didn't get cheated out of tips by people ordering at the bar and then taking their own drinks to the tables. Bernie was headed out back.

He pushed open the door to the employee entrance. Nobody else was around since this wasn't exactly rush hour for the casino. A few men in white jackets worked on food prep for the evening dinner service, but they ignored Bernie and kept peeling potatoes, washing fruit, and scrubbing pots.

He walked quickly, knowing he was already two minutes late to the meeting, if his watch were correct. He pushed through the rear door and was met by the sour stench of the garbage dumpsters.

The guy had said to meet around back, but he hadn't specified where. Bernie moved away from the garbage and scanned the lot for the guy. He had no idea how he would stall without the money. He thought maybe he would haggle more about price. He could make a show of inspecting the girl and acting unsatisfied, but he didn't want them to just pack up and leave before the law got there.

He didn't see the guy from the bar or Concho. He tilted his hand to check his watch and spilled beer from the neck of his bottle.

"Aw, crap," he said.

* * *

CONCHO EASED INTO THE PARKING LOT, CHECKING EVERY CAR and every person he saw. He rolled slowly through the lot and around to the back of the casino. He'd never been back there. For all the artifice and fake glamour out front, the back of the building was very utilitarian.

A loading dock, a fire lane, dumpsters, an air conditioning unit the size of a small house.

He drove to the far corner, the end of a long line of employee cars, and parked. He decided not to wear his ranger badge. He didn't want to scare away the man selling the girl. He needed to see this for himself and figure out if it was legit. He kept his gun on him, though.

Concho walked toward the building, checking the parked cars, the edge of the lot, any place someone could hide. He spotted Bernie walking around behind the building and looking lost. He was alone.

Concho whistled once and Bernie looked up. He seemed to relax when he saw it was Concho. Bernie waved him over.

"He hasn't shown," Bernie said, flipping his wrist over to check his watch.

"Think it was all a bunch of BS?" Concho asked.

"He seemed pretty serious about it. Not much of a prank. If he wanted to get me alone with the ten grand and then rob me, that I get."

"He's only a minute or two late," Concho said. "Let's give him fifteen minutes."

"Okay." Bernie let out a long breath. Concho could smell the beer. "Sure am glad to see you, Concho."

"Thanks for the call." Concho felt glad he didn't call for backup. It looked like a bust. Either a prank, or a figment of Bernie's alcohol-addled brain. But he had fifteen minutes to give it to make sure.

* * *

CONSUELA'S BARE FEET BURNED ON THE BLACKTOP. SHE WOULD have been running anyway to keep her feet from burning. She took short, hopping steps and aimed for the tan sandy scrub at the edge of the lot.

Rubén gained ground on her quickly. He resisted yelling at her because he didn't want to draw any attention to them. There were no cars to dodge so he made a straight line at her and grabbed ahold of her arm at the elbow when he reached her. She yanked her arm away and veered left. He nearly rolled his ankle when he tried to turn to chase her. She got another several steps ahead of him with her juke, but he caught up again. She dodged away, using moves learned from years of *fútbol* playing. Rubén stumbled as he tried to match her moves.

Hugo watched from the car and saw his partner bob and weave, but not catch the girl as she serpentined away across the lot.

He reached close enough to touch her hair, then dodged. The next time he brushed her back, but she cut left. They weren't going fast, but Rubén panted for air as the change of directions burned his lungs.

Consuela knew she couldn't get away. There was nowhere

to go here. She should have run for the casino doors right
away, but the whole place was so new and strange and fright-
ening to her. She had no idea if this casino was owned by The
Black Wolf. If she walked inside begging for help, was she
walking into trouble?

She could feel blisters rising on her feet from the heat. She
cut right and stumbled, scraping the side of her foot. She
thought for a second she might go down and thrust out her
hands and had to slow down to stay upright. Rubén was right
behind her and grabbed at her elbow again.

Consuela screeched and tried to pull away, but he held
firm. He slowed his pace and brought her to a halt. He didn't
say anything while he tried to catch his breath.

Consuela stepped from foot to foot, lifting one and then the
other off the hot tarmac.

"Don't try that again," Rubén said. "Now come on."

He began dragging her back to the car.

Hugo sat in the passenger seat with his legs out of the car
and rubbed his chin. Her kick had caught solidly and he
wondered if she had broken something. It still hurt like hell.

Rubén came walking up with Consuela in his grip. He set
her down in the backseat.

"So untying her was a mistake," Rubén said between heavy
breaths.

"You think he'll mind if she's tied up?"

"The guy is buying another person. I don't think he cares a
whole lot."

"Yeah. maybe not. Okay, tie her up again. I'll drive us
around back and park far away. C'mon, we're already late."

* * *

CONCHO CLOCKED THE CAR AS IT PULLED INTO THE BACKLOT.
It moved slowly and went to the end of the line near where he
had parked. If it was an employee, they'd know soon enough.

"Is that them?" Concho asked.

Bernie squinted at the car. "I'm not sure. Didn't get a good look."

Concho moved his gun around to the small of his back, out of sight. They waited and after a minute, the same guy from the bar walked toward them.

"That's him," Bernie said.

Hugo stopped about twenty feet away. "Who's this?"

Concho said, "You didn't think he could get all that money on his own, did you?"

"He's my business partner," Bernie said.

Hugo stayed where he was, a dubious look on his face.

"You got the girl?" Concho asked. He needed to put eyes on her before he thought about busting them. If he brought this guy down, but the girl wasn't here, chances were slim he could find her. If she was even real.

"You got the cash?" Hugo said.

"I'd like to see what I'm buying first."

Hugo nodded like that was fair. "Okay, hold on." He turned and waved his arm over his head. He turned back. "One second."

"Where's she from?" Concho asked.

"Mexico."

"Can you get more? I might have some more interested parties." If this girl wasn't the one who was taken on the Rez, then this might be part of a larger trafficking operation. Concho wanted to cover his bases. Right then he regretted not calling in backup.

"Maybe," Hugo said. "This first one is a discount, though. You want more, it'll cost you…twenty."

To Concho, the guy was clearly making this up as he went along. This was no seasoned abduction operation. The way he asked for more was like a kid asking for seconds of ice cream.

"We'll see how this one works out first," Concho said.

A second man approached, walking a girl with him. His hand was clamped tight on her arm and her hands were bound together. Her feet were bare and she looked both scared and pissed off.

Hugo smiled. "Nice, right?"

"She speak English?"

"You really want to talk to her? Whatever, man. It's your money. I can think of better things to do."

Concho walked toward them. Hugo and Rubén both flinched but held their ground.

"She healthy?" Concho asked. He needed to get a closer look.

"Healthy where it counts," Hugo said. "Now, where's that money?"

"I got it in chips. We'll go inside and cash them in at the cages. You get whatever denominations you want. Already been laundered by going through the casino."

Hugo smiled like it had been his brilliant idea all along. "Yeah, sweet."

Concho had seen enough. He looked at the girl, saw the fear in her eyes. "You come from the Rez?"

The question confused her at first. Then she slowly nodded. "Si."

"Is your mama's name Faustina?"

The girl's eyes went wide. "Si!"

Conch nodded once and reached behind his back. He brought the gun around and said, "Stay right there. Texas Ranger."

Rubén didn't wait. He shoved Consuela forward, crashing her into Concho, and he sprinted for the back door of the Lucky Eagle.

CHAPTER FORTY-TWO

HANG ON TO THE GUN, THOUGHT CONCHO AS HE FELL. HE might have been able to keep himself upright if he'd let it go, but giving away his pistol to one of these men was not an option. He hit the blacktop hard on his side and grunted. He could hear footsteps fading away from him.

Hugo saw Rubén dash away toward the back door of the casino, saw the stranger with a gun hit the ground and thought, *screw this*. Hugo ran away from the building, headed for the car.

Bernie watched the whole thing with his jaw hung open. At least it was real and not just a gag. The new guy was sprinting toward him and Concho was down. Bernie knew he had to do something. He moved and put his body in the path between the runner and the back door to the kitchen. He held his arms out wide like he was defending a receiver in a game of backyard football. Rubén came at him like a pro ball player.

Rubén never broke stride as he wound back his arm and swung at Bernie. The punch clipped Bernie across his chin and spun him in a full circle. By the time Bernie hit the ground, Rubén was already past him and pulling at the door.

Concho got to one knee. He saw each man going in opposite directions. The one who'd shoved him was headed inside the casino where he could cause more trouble. He had to pick, so he chose to follow Rubén.

Consuela was standing wrapped in her own arms, stunned and shaking. The burning on her feet was the least of her problems now. Concho stood and went to work on the loose knot holding her hands together.

"You're okay now," he said. "See that truck at the end of this line of parking spaces?"

He pointed and she nodded. He dropped the rope on the ground. She was free now.

"That's my truck. Go there and wait for me. Stay out of sight. Okay? *Entender?*"

"Si." She wanted to ask for the gun, but she turned and ran toward the truck.

* * *

Rubén burst through the kitchen door and took a second to take in where he was. Pots and pans, steel countertops, men and women in white jackets and bandanas on their heads. A kitchen. He bolted forward.

To his right, he saw a rack of knives adhered to the wall by a magnetic strip. He stopped, doubled back, and grabbed a long chef's knife from the row. He charged forward again.

The woman on potato peeling duty watched all this, a half-peeled spud in her hand. When the stranger snatched a knife off the wall she panicked. When he came running her way, she used the only weapon she had near. She reared back and hurled the fist-sized potato at the running man. Years of playing in the backyard with her three brothers had given her quite the arm and accurate aim. The potato hit Rubén on the bridge of his nose. Unboiled, the potato was hard as a rock and it opened up a cut in his skin. Blood began to flow down his face, but he never broke stride.

He saw the swinging door out onto the floor of the casino.

Keeping a lookout for more flying potatoes, he angled toward the door.

* * *

CONCHO REACHED WHERE BERNIE STILL LAY ON THE GROUND. He bent down to him.

"You okay?" Concho asked.

Bernie rubbed his head and moaned.

"Listen, call Echabarri. Tell him to get down here and bring backup. You got me?"

Bernie moaned again. "Yeah, yeah, I'll call him."

"Good. Fill him in on the whole thing. Do it now."

Concho left Bernie to it and went to the back door. He pushed through, gun at the ready.

The kitchen workers were gathered together in a group, discussing what had just happened. They all turned when the new man entered and they all saw his gun. A few let out screams. Concho dug in his pocket for his ranger badge and held it out in front of his like a talisman.

"Texas Ranger. Where did he go?"

As one, the ground pointed to the swinging door. Concho nodded his thanks and ran after him. A chef called out, "He's got a knife."

* * *

IT STARTED TO SINK IN TO CONSUELA THAT SHE WAS FREE NOW. She slowed her pace as much as her feet would allow as she got closer to the truck. She wouldn't truly feel safe until she was back across the border and in the arms of her mother, but she knew how truly lucky she was.

She reached the large white F-150 and looked around for a place to hide. She decided the bed of the truck would be the best place. Out of sight, off the hot asphalt and she could lay down finally.

She put her hands on the side and put one foot on the back tires to boost herself. Then she felt hands on her, pulling her back.

* * *

HUGO HAD ALMOST BEEN TO HIS CAR, READY TO DRIVE AWAY and leave Rubén to his fate. He knew he would have to run. You didn't screw up a job for The Black Wolf and James Lee Morris and merely apologize. He'd go back south to Mexico, leave the border area. Go deep south into Chiapas or Campeche.

Then he saw the girl.

She was the cause of all this. Sure, his greed played a part, but she had been the root of this disaster. Maybe James Lee had it right from the start. Get rid of her and be done with it. He hadn't been able to find the courage before, but now his anger and his desire not to be on the run for the rest of his life, gave him a new courage. He turned away from his own car and crossed the row of parked cars to where she was trying to climb into a pickup truck.

* * *

CONSUELA TURNED AND SAW HUGO. SHE WAS TOO CLOSE TO freedom. She would not let him take her back.

When she was first taken, all the stories of all the other girls were in her head. She knew she was doomed. She barely fought back because what was the use? But now, she had tasted freedom and it was still sweet on her tongue.

She bared her teeth. She twisted her body and ripped her arms from his grip. She reached out and grabbed his hair with both hands. She pulled his head toward her and down as she brought her knee up and hit him in the center of his face with as much force as she could muster. She felt his nose give way.

Consuela jerked him back up and the blood had already

started flowing from his nostrils. Keeping hold of his hair, she turned him and smashed his face into the chrome bumper of the F-150. More blood came spurting out. Hugo made a noise from the back of his throat. His head lolled to the side, already half-unconscious.

She pulled at him again and rammed the crown of his skull into the Ford logo on the front of the truck. Hugo went limp and she let him fall to the ground. She quickly went to the bed of the truck and found a bungee cord with a hook on each end. She came back and tied his arms behind his back, then tied his feet together, but not before removing his shoes and tossing them into the dirt by the fence.

Consuela dragged Hugo around to the rear bumper of the truck and sat him up out of sight. He moaned and tried to lift his head, but his brain was too foggy. She spit on him, then stepped one foot on his shoulder and used him as a step to climb into the bed of the truck to wait for Concho's return.

* * *

RUBÉN NEEDED A MINUTE TO ORIENT HIMSELF. HE'D NEVER been inside the Lucky Eagle before and it was like they hid the exit doors. No clocks, no windows, and the pattern on the carpet was like a melted maze where all paths lead back to the start. They didn't want you to leave here.

Knife in hand, he ran, weaving between tables and eliciting screams from the cocktail waitresses. When the first scream rose above the noise of the slot machines, he regretted not trying to slip out quietly. Stow the knife and just walk calmly to the exit, but he panicked. A man standing at the roulette wheel scooped up his chips and ran, leaving his bet on the table with the wheel still spinning.

Rubén bumped the edge of the blackjack table with his hip. The table rocked, spilling a pile of chips the man in the center seat had placed beside his hand. The dealer, a short woman with long black hair tied in twin braids, ducked behind the table. Rubén passed by quickly and the man at the table reached over and grabbed a fistful of hundred-dollar chips while the dealer was crawling on the floor away from the weirdo with the knife.

Casino security was on alert now. Two beefy men in suits and ties with tasers tucked under their jackets started moving in from opposite sides of the room. Rubén saw one of them lock eyes on him. He reached over to the stack of chips at the roulette wheel and scooped up as much as he could hold. The dealer ran the other way. Rubén tossed the chips in an arc, spraying the room with twenties, fifties, and hundreds.

The patrons were torn. A man with a knife was running around, but there was money falling from the sky.

Rubén saw the entrance to the theater with the nightly dance show and cover band. It was empty now, hours before showtime, but it was a doorway and he ran for it.

* * *

CONCHO CAME THROUGH THE KITCHEN DOOR AND ONTO THE casino floor just in time to see Rubén toss the chips into the air. He angled that way. When Rubén left the gaming floor and headed toward the theater, patrons who had been at tables were now on their hands and knees, grabbing for fallen chips like starving animals.

Concho clocked the two security guards tailing after Rubén. He met them at the edge of the gaming floor and held out his badge.

"Concho Ten-Wolves, Texas Ranger. What's down here?"

"The theater," one beefy guard said. The other had his eyes on the patrons stealing chips.

"Is there a back way out of there?"

"There's a stage door and a roll-up door for loading in sets and the band equipment."

"You get around back. If he comes out, stop him."

"Got it."

He sprinted away. His partner held back a moment, watching the theft going on in plain sight, but figured a lunatic with a knife was a higher priority. He followed his partner.

Concho pocketed his badge and let his gun lead the way down a short hall and into the theater.

CHAPTER FORTY-THREE

The room sat about three hundred. Utility lights were on, but nothing else. The room was dim and shadowy, the rows of seats in red velvet offered a hundred different hiding places. Concho waited at the door and listened. Hunting and tracking, he'd learned as a young boy, were as much about stillness as the chase. Meskwaa had given him lessons in being still, training his mind to focus on one thing only – a sound, a smell, the feeling the ground beneath your feet. It worked well for hunting mule deer and coyotes, but they were wary of predators and trying not to get caught. The man Concho was after now was desperate, inexperienced, and scared.

He heard him right away.

Rubén dashed out from the shadows and ran up the short steps on the side of the stage. When his feet hit the boards of the stage, he might as well have had tap shoes on.

Concho raised his gun. "Hold it right there. Texas Ranger."

Rubén cut a quick glance over his shoulder at Concho, but he didn't stop.

The band's instruments were set up, awaiting the night's show. A piano, a drum riser with a full kit, three chairs and music stands for the horns, plus amplifiers and monitors. Rubén ran for the back of the stage and lost himself in the maze of equipment. Concho lost him behind the drum kit.

Concho charged down the center aisle and vaulted himself onto the stage in a leap, bypassing the steps entirely. Rubén was pushing his way through the tangle of cables and cords. He tripped, stumbled and pulled over a cymbal which crashed to the stage with a cacophony.

"Freeze!" Concho said.

Rubén spun and flung the knife toward the voice. Concho ducked sideways and the blade sailed over his left shoulder, so close it sliced through several of Concho's long hairs which fell to the stage.

Rubén plowed over an amplifier like he was a fullback and leaped off the back of the stage. A red EXIT sign glowed up ahead.

Concho had to dodge the dense thicket of musical equipment to follow. He was reluctant to fire any shots and do any damage that wasn't necessary. The longer the chase went on, though, the itchier his trigger finger became.

He could hear the panicked grunts and panting of Rubén as he kept up the run far longer than he had the lungs for. Rubén made a lunge for the EXIT door and pushed the bar, exposing a blinding rectangle of daylight into the darkened theater.

Rubén was met by a taser being thrust into his ribs. As he stood straight and convulsed, a second taser was pressed against his neck. Concho heard the crackle of the charge and heard Rubén's jaw-clenching grunts as he took the shock. After a full three seconds, the two tasers lifted off his body and Rubén collapsed to the floor.

Concho stepped up behind the prone figure and saw the two security guards looking quite pleased with themselves.

"Thanks, guys."

One of the beefy men hefted the taser in his hand. "I always wanted to use this thing."

* * *

A HALF HOUR LATER ECHABARRI SHOOK HANDS WITH THE TWO
security guards, thanked them and pointed them to where a
uniformed officer was waiting. He turned and looked at
Concho across the casino floor, then shook his head. He walked
to where Concho was sitting at an empty blackjack table. The
chips had all been removed from this and every table on the
floor. Gaming was done for the next few hours, though they
had been getting pressure from the management to clear out as
soon as they could so the games could begin again. Talk would
spread all over the Rez about the craziness at the Lucky Eagle
and that meant a bump in visitors for the next few days.

Echabarri leaned one elbow on the green felt top of the
table.

"Do I even want to know about the guy hog-tied in the bed
of your truck?"

"Did you ask her about it?"

"We did. Her story fits with yours. And Bernie."

Echabarri nodded toward the bar where Bernie sat in his
usual seat, now surrounded by curious listeners as he recounted
his bravery and heroism.

"Well, the whole thing fits with my case against this Black
Wolf guy," Concho said. "Not quite sure why this girl was
trying to be unloaded instead of going up to the prison like the
others, but either way, I'm going to bust him and make sure
this was the last girl."

"Oh, the one you tased had a story about that."

Concho held up his hands. "I didn't tase anyone."

"Right," Echabarri said. He gave a slight tilt of his head
toward Concho's sidearm. "Taser's too weak for you. Anyway,
this guy said they had plans to bring the girl north, but they got
called off. They were supposed to kill her and dump her in the
desert. He's trying to spin it like they were doing a good thing
by selling her to Bernie."

Concho thought on this. Why would they call off the delivery of the new girl?

"I gotta check in with Shaw and see if we're cleared to go get this guy."

Echabarri leaned both elbows on the table now. "How do you bust a guy who's already in prison?"

"No idea. But I'm about to find out."

* * *

A DARK FIGURE LIKE A PERCHING CROW SAT ON CONCHO'S front step. As he slid out of the truck, he could tell it was Meskwaa on an unusual house call. The old shaman had always made Concho come to him in the past.

He sat with his eyes closed, face turned toward the low sun. Concho thought he might be asleep but without opening his eyes, he said, "Your house faces the wrong way."

"It does?"

He opened his tired, red-rimmed eyes. "You can choose to face the rising sun if you wish to start the day in light, or you can face the setting sun if you wish to end the day in contemplation of what you have achieved that day. But to face south, where you can see the sun move along the sky all day, you spend more of your day marking time than living."

"Well, I'm rarely here, so it doesn't really bother me."

"You are one who does not follow the sun? You prefer the *anaakwa*."

Concho looked up to the sky. "Yes, I like the stars. I like that they're there all the time even when we can't see them."

"Like the clues in your work. Truths merely waiting to be discovered."

"I suppose. Is that why you came here? To tell me my house was facing the wrong direction?"

Meskwaa tapped his forehead. "I had a vision."

"About me?"

"You weren't in it, but when it ended, I had a strong feeling of you."

"What was the vision?"

"An eagle leaving the nest. It flew away, and there was blood on the talons."

Concho waited for more. "That's it?"

Meskwaa nodded.

"What do you think it means?" Concho asked.

"That is the feeling I got that brought me to you. That you would know where I did not. Perhaps because you don't make yourself available to the visions as you should. I received a vision meant for you."

Concho didn't know what it meant. "Come inside," he said. "I'll make you some food before I take you home."

"There was blood on the wings as well."

"Sounds like a bad omen, whatever it is."

"Blood isn't always bad. Blood gives life."

"Not in my line of work."

He stepped next to the old man and helped him to his feet, then held the door open as he shuffled inside.

CHAPTER FORTY-FOUR

A GUARD NAMED MOSBY APPROACHED THE CELL WARILY. AFTER what happened to Roy, even the guards on the take were afraid of what The Black Wolf might do, or have his men do, if he turned out to be in a foul mood.

As he crested the top step Mosby could see two henchmen holding a blanket shoulder height between them, shielding The Black Wolf as he sat on the toilet. Private facilities were out of the realm of payoffs and influence, but he could still enjoy some measure of privacy with the help of his loyal men.

One of the most loyal, Tito, stood in the cell's doorway. Mosby approached.

"Tell him it's on for tomorrow, seven a.m."

Tito smiled with half his mouth. "Tell him yourself."

Mosby coughed once, then raised his voice. "It's Mosby. We're on for tomorrow at seven a.m."

The Black Wolf's voice came from behind the blanket. "Everything has been arranged?"

"That's James Lee's problem. All I know is he told me to tell you tomorrow at seven."

Mosby took the silence as approval.

Tito tapped Mosby on the shoulder. "You gonna miss your monthly envelopes?"

"Honestly? Not so much. Makes me nervous. My stomach's been jumping cartwheels for months."

Tito scoffed. "Who are you afraid of? Scalise? He's as weak as the coffee they serve in this joint."

Mosby shook his head vigorously. "It ain't the warden I'm afraid of."

Tito pointed over his shoulder to the blanket and behind it, The Black Wolf. "Him?"

"You saw what happened to Roy. Hell, I wasn't here, but for all I know, you tossed him over."

"Let me tell you, my friend." Tito put an arm around Mosby's shoulder like they were old pals. He tightened it until the crook of his elbow pinched the back of Mosby's neck. "All you need to do is not make any mistakes and you won't go over the edge." Tito pointed to where Roy had been thrown and made a high whistle through his teeth. "And you know, even when he's gone, he still has eyes and ears all around this place."

"You don't gotta worry about me."

Tito patted him on the chest and released his arm from around Mosby's neck. "I never do."

Mosby scurried away, chased by the sound of the toilet flushing. The blanket was lowered and The Black Wolf stepped forward, cinching up his belt.

"My last night here," he said.

The others nodded and smiled at the good news.

"I don't want to leave any unfinished business."

The Black Wolf looked out over the cell block from his perch on the second level.

"Is Witten still in solitary?"

Tito nodded.

"Walk with me."

* * *

SOLITARY CONFINEMENT WAS A SINGLE HALL OF CELLS, SIX TO A side. Rarely were they all full. Only four were occupied now. The walls were dark cinderblock and the floor dark concrete. The doors to the cells had only a thin rectangle cut into them that slid open for delivering serving trays. Inside the cells only a tiny window high off the floor gave any light.

Scalise didn't send many men here, and when he did they seldom stayed for long. The Black Wolf had been waiting for Witten's release back into general population, but the accelerated break-out schedule had made a visit to the dim hallway necessary.

Only one guard had run of the row of cells. His name was Kardin. A short man with a sharp angled nose and buzz haircut, he obeyed orders from The Black Wolf for only pennies what he had to pay the others. The man had no business being a guard for the kind of men who were sent to live at Bigfoot. He would have had trouble establishing authority over a class of fifth graders.

Tito stepped into the doorway of the small cube where Kardin sat all day reading magazines and comic books. The Black Wolf loomed behind, and behind him, his two blanket-holding friends. Tito snapped his fingers once and said, "Witten."

Kardin swallowed hard. "Uh, three. Number three."

Tito held out an open hand as an invitation. Kardin put a key into it, then went back to his magazine, ignoring what he knew was about to happen.

Tito led the way and unlocked cell number three. Witten was sleeping on the cot bolted to the wall. Aside from it and a dull silver toilet with no lid, the room was bare. He blinked his eyes a few times, then saw Tito move out of the way and The Black Wolf filled the doorway.

Witten scrambled into the corner of the bed, clutching the thin blanket with him as if it might offer some protection. He had been a high school athlete. Bound for a college scholarship, they say, before he got a taste for the drugs he was dealing out of his locker.

Now his rail-thin limbs looked better for running a marathon than pounding it out on the line in a football game. Witten was new to Bigfoot. He had crossed The Black Wolf without even knowing it. He had a beef with one of his men. Things he said about The Black Wolf had gotten back to him. He was offered a chance to apologize and, not realizing the power of the man, had refused. The ensuing beat down had landed him in solitary.

"Unfinished business," The Black Wolf said.

"Huh?"

The Black Wolf took a step inside. He undid and then removed his belt. The same one he had just cinched back onto his body. He held it out like a limp snake for Witten to see.

"I'm offering you a choice," he said.

"W–what choice?" Witten continued to cower in the corner.

"Between what comes when you get out of this cell. Or having your fate in your own hands."

Witten squeezed the blanket tighter. "I don't…I don't know what you mean."

"You know what will happen to you when you join the others." He turned slightly to acknowledge the men behind him. Witten watched them nervously. "So I offer you a way out."

He extended his hand with the belt. The brown leather swayed as it hung from his hand.

Witten pointed at the belt. "You mean…?"

"It will be much less painful, I promise you. *Much* less."

The Black Wolf stood still, his arm held out, eyes locked on Witten's.

"I ain't got a choice?"

"Oh, this is a choice. The result is the same, but make no mistake, I am offering you mercy."

"How 'bout I apologize. I didn't know. I'm green. I don't

know squat about this place, who is in it. Who you is. I didn't
know and I'm sorry. Damn, sorry."

The Black Wolf seemed as if he hadn't even heard the
words. "Please decide. My arm is getting tired."

Witten looked from Tito and the men to The Black Wolf,
to the belt in his hand. He thought about it. Tears began dripping from his eyes.

He reached out, tentatively at first. He had to tilt his body
forward and go on his knees to reach the belt. He took it and it
slid off of The Black Wolf's hand.

"If you don't. If you are unable, they will still be waiting
for you when you get out."

The Black Wolf turned his back on Witten and left, Tito
and the boys parting to let him pass.

Witten sat on his cot, the belt in his hand, crying. It would
be his last night behind bars too.

CHAPTER FORTY-FIVE

The phone rang and Concho tapped the speaker button since he was driving after dropping Meskwaa off at his home. It was Dalton Shaw on the line and he didn't want to miss the call.

"Hey."

"We're all set," Shaw said. "DEA of course wants to get involved since he's a whale for them. Corrections department officials will be there too to hopefully handle the bad guards. Not sure how much was can clean out all in one sweep, but the guy said they're bringing in some temps to put in place depending on how many guys we can get for looking the other way."

"Gotta be some assets. Maybe we can claw back? Money they took over the years?"

"Whatever disciplinary course of action they want to take, I'll let them deal with it. Frankly, I'm eager to get this case off my desk and get you back to work in this office."

"Me too," Concho said. "You coming up with me?"

Shaw laughed into the phone. "I have real responsibilities in my own office. You remember that, right? Company D?

Based in Weslaco? Or did you forget since you haven't been here in so damn long?"

Concho smiled, knowing the boss was toying with him. "Can't get rid of me," he said. "I'm like one of those dogs who finds its way back home after the family moves out to California or something."

"Yeah, well you get tomorrow to wrap this up and then that's it. I want to see you at your desk the day after."

"No can do."

There was a pause. "Why the hell not?"

"That's a Saturday, chief."

Shaw seemed in no mood for games. "You know what the hell I mean, Ten-Wolves. Butt in seat the next work day. Get me?"

"Got it."

Shaw hung up without a goodbye. It timed out that Concho was just pulling into home when the call ended. For the second time he found someone waiting for him. This time it was Maria. As much as he enjoyed visiting with the old shaman, he knew this visit would be more to his liking.

* * *

WARDEN FRANK SCALISE SHUT THE DOOR TO HIS HOME BEHIND him and ran a hand over his thinning hair. He didn't know how much longer he could take being at the prison. He so often felt like he was just as locked up as the inmates. He knew it was foolish, but the place was designed to keep men in and to remind them that they had limits, loss of freedom, restraint. Even if he could leave the high walls every day and come home, it added up and drained him.

Now with what happened to Roy, and no one saying a word about who was responsible, the pressure was building.

Debra came from the kitchen wiping her hands on a dish towel.

"Hi, dear."

"Hi, honey."

They shared a passionless kiss and he slumped to the couch where he would stay planted for the rest of the evening.

"I made pasta," Debra said.

"Sounds good." He lifted the remote and turned on the TV, not sure what he was in the mood for.

Debra stopped before returning to the kitchen. "You okay, hon? You seem low."

"Don't I seem low every day when I get home?"

"Lower than usual, then." She tried to smile and perk him up, but he wasn't having it. "Jeez, you are low."

Scalise powered off the TV. "It's just…am I a weak man?"

"Well, you can't do pushups like you used to do."

He squirmed in his seat, getting anxious. "Not physically weak. I mean weak of character."

"Frank Scalise, you are not weak of character."

"Sometimes I wonder."

Debra sat on the arm of the couch and folded the dish towel in her lap. "What brought this on? Is it that guard who got killed?"

"It's that. It's all of it." He didn't want to tell her anymore about The Black Wolf. She'd seen too much when James Lee had invaded their home. Frank made some excuses and explained a little, but kept her in the dark about most of it. He felt foolish. He'd been trying to straddle the line between right and wrong. Not taking money, but turning a blind eye. Keeping the peace by staying out of it.

"I just wonder," he said, "If this job is getting the best of me. Maybe it's time for a change."

"Lord knows you've earned it. Our savings might disagree, though."

"I know."

Debra slid down and sat next to him. She took his hand in hers. "You need to do what makes you happy. We'll figure the rest out. You've put in twenty good years there. Nobody can blame you if you wanted a change."

"I'm too young to retire."

"You're too young to give up and stay with a job you don't love anymore." She lifted his hand to her mouth and kissed it. "And I'll be honest, the idea of you not being out there with those scary men anymore would make me sleep more soundly at night."

He squeezed her hand.

"I don't know what I'll do, but something's got to change."

"Have some spaghetti. You'll feel better on a full stomach."

She stood and dragged him up with her.

"This is why I can't do those pushups anymore."

Debra chuckled at that and finally he smiled.

CHAPTER FORTY-SIX

JAMES LEE KNEW A PHONE CALL THIS EARLY COULDN'T BE GOOD news. He answered it anyway.

"We got a problem."

So he'd been right. Bad news. Everything was in place for The Black Wolf's break-out. A simple plan, executed simply and then he was out. His last ride with the boss. Not as many protections in place as he would have liked, but he'd go down over the border, collect his payment and then on a plane to the islands. But there was always a problem.

"Not what I want to hear," James Lee said.

One of the four guards on his payroll was calling. One of the four needed to make the plan work. Opening doors, bypassing gates, until The Black Wolf was outside the walls and into one of the black SUVs waiting for him. James Lee checked the clock by his bedside. Six twenty-two a.m.

"Garver called in sick."

"What do you mean sick?"

"I don't know. He called in sick. He got Simmons to cover his shift. He'll be here at seven."

James Lee pinched the bridge of his nose. "Sick with what? Cold feet? Damn it."

"Simmons said he needs to drop his kid off at school and then he'd be in. Could we move it up to before he gets here?"

"Nah, not enough time."

James Lee had been about to leave his house. He'd packed what he wanted to take with him and made arrangements for it to be shipped to him once he landed wherever he would end up. The plan was flexible and the timeline could be moved, but three men made it next to impossible to get The Black Wolf out the doors. Garver had been the last man in the line. The door to the outside. Without one of their men on that crucial final step, nobody was leaving the prison.

It wasn't too late for him to bail too. Just say screw it and leave the boss in prison, where he belonged. But that final payoff was too good to leave behind. He needed to think.

"What do we do?" the guard asked.

"Gimme a minute."

He didn't know this Simmons, didn't know if he could be bought on the spot. The cash would have to come from James Lee's own money, hopefully to be paid back but with no guarantee. And Simmons would be in a strong position for bargaining.

"What do you know about this guy?" James Lee asked.

"Simmons? Good guy. Straight arrow. A family man, been here like twelve years."

"Can he be bought?"

"I wouldn't count on it."

"Damn it."

James Lee checked the clock again, thought over what he'd been told. A spark of an idea came to him. It wasn't ideal, he didn't like it much, but it was all he had.

"Tell everyone to hold. I'll be a little late, but we're still a go. Just need to make a stop first."

James Lee hung up. He'd compromised himself for years now, turned his back on a lifetime of following rules and obeying orders. What was one more crime to add to the list?

* * *

CONCHO WAS UP EARLY. HE ATE BREAKFAST, HAD COFFEE, DID some pushups and scattered the remnants of a stale end of bread in the yard for the birds.

Shaw had given him the names and contact numbers for the members of the other departments he was to meet near the prison. They decided not to contact Warden Scalise ahead of time since nobody could determine his exact involvement with The Black Wolf. They didn't know what he could do about it if he knew they were coming that day, but they didn't want to risk it. About the only thing the warden could do would be to sneak The Black Wolf out of the prison, but nobody thought that was a serious threat.

Maria stepped into the kitchen and poured herself a cup of coffee.

"Today's the big day, huh?"

"Yep."

"So after this I get you back full time?"

"You should." He finished the last of his coffee and set the cup in the sink. "I guess it's true what they say that absence makes the heart grow fonder."

"If that's really true then you should love the hell out of me right now."

He smiled at her. "You know I do."

Maria pulled him into a kiss that lasted a good long while. When they pulled apart, she tilted her eyes down to the sink and said, "You just gonna leave that cup there?"

"Sorry. Duty calls." With a smile, Concho was out the door.

* * *

NOT NORMALLY A MORNING PERSON, THE BLACK WOLF WAS awake. He sat on his bunk with his hands on his knees, waiting. The rest of the cell block was still quiet. Only a few early risers.

In only a short time, though, the block would be buzzing and echoing with cons waking and talking and acting like all this was normal.

He himself had grown to think of it as a form of normal. He knew it was the only way to cope inside. Now that he was on the verge of getting out, he felt angry for ever allowing himself to think this way of life as anything approaching normal.

As a boy, when The Black Wolf was still known as Fulgencio Labante, he attended a Catholic school in Mexico. The nuns wore black habits with skirts that fell all the way to the floor, long bunches of fabric that hid their arms with only an oval cut into the wimple to show their pinched and sour faces. They spent all day with a ruler in one hand ready to dole out punishment to anyone who needed it. For committing the sin of being a child.

They rapped knuckles, twisted earlobes, spanked bottoms with paddles engraved with crosses. The kids knew no different. They all thought it was normal.

One day, young Fulgencio was late coming in from recess. A nun went out to the yard to retrieve him and found him urinating in the tomato patch. As he was dragged back to class, he argued that he had to go, it was an emergency. The sister didn't care for his excuses. When she got him to class, she shut him in the closet and told him to pray.

Whether it was part of the punishment or she merely forgot, Fulgencio spent the rest of the day in that closet. The bell in the tower rang and classes ended. The other children went home. He stayed inside, praying in silence, waiting for release.

An hour after the children had left, the nun went to the closet to retrieve something and gasped when the boy was there. She tried to cover the fact that she had forgotten him, but he could see it in her surprise.

She told him to pray for forgiveness of his sin before bed

and when he returned to school the next day, he would be forgiven by God.

Fulgencio didn't say a word. He left and walked home.

It was his first imprisonment. He knew no different. The nuns ran the school. It was all normal to him.

When he was older, just beginning to make his empire of crime, he finally understood that it was not normal at all to lock a child in a closet for hours with no food or water.

He vowed never to let anyone treat him like that again. Never to see it as normal.

Tito arrived at his cell door. He could see The Black Wolf was deep in thought so he waited. When The Black Wolf looked his way, he said, "There is a delay."

The Black Wolf's hands tightened on his knees. His knuckles went white.

"How long?"

"Not sure, but not long. James Lee said he's on it."

The Black Wolf nodded slowly, then turned his neck until it cracked. He tilted his head to the other side where there were more pops. He settled back into position and waited. He did not pray this time.

CHAPTER FORTY-SEVEN

CONCHO DROVE NORTHEAST ON HIGHWAY FIFTY-SEVEN, TWO lanes of blacktop surrounded by ranches and low scrub brush. The air had turned warmer, summer not far off. Concho had the window down and his arm propped up in the open space, sun heating his skin. He'd known truck drivers with deep lines and wrinkles on the left side of their faces, left arms deep brown and spotted from years of driving with an open window. The right sides of their bodies that stayed in the shade and protection of the truck cab were half as lined, much more pale.

He'd be glad to put this one behind him. He had to admit, it felt good. It wasn't always you saw the direct impact of what he did. When stopping the bad guys meant preventing a future crime, the victims of which he'd never know, it still meant something but wasn't quite as visceral as seeing what bringing those girls back home meant to a family and a community.

Arrangements were being made to get Consuela back home, but her case involved her being a witness against two living suspects. Unlike the dead man who had hold of Ximena.

Whenever it was approved, Concho had already requested Shaw to escort her home. Maybe he'd bring Maria this time, show her the party that awaited.

A jackrabbit bolted from the bushes and shot across the two-lane like he'd been fired from a sniper rifle. Concho didn't have time to brake before the jackrabbit was there and then gone, bounding off into the brush on the other side of the highway.

The road led out in front of him ruler-straight and flat as a bowling lane. The sandy shoulders were like gutters. High white clouds hung overhead, not moving in a cornflower blue sky.

Concho turned north on Eighty-Three through Uvalde and then onto Fifty-Five for more north. He'd barely passed another car on the road and made good time. He'd be at Bigfoot before breakfast was served in the mess hall.

* * *

JAMES LEE SAT IN THE BACK SEAT OF THE SECOND IN A LINE OF four black Lincoln Navigators with Mexican plates. The little detour had taken him nearly an hour, first to get the information he needed, then to execute the new part of the plan. He knew that meant The Black Wolf would have words for him when he finally joined him in the back seat of the Navigator, but James Lee would assure him it wasn't his fault and would even be able to impress him with how well and how quickly he improvised a solution.

Unless it all falls apart and doesn't work. Then he'd be lucky to escape with his life and still make it to the islands on half the cash he had been counting on. No way to find out if it would work other than to try it.

He sent a text message:

BRING HIM NOW.

Then another.

LET ME KNOW WHEN HE GETS TO THE LAST GATE. ONE WITH SIMMONS.

He waited, ignoring the small whimpers and cries from the seat next to him.

* * *

Mosby walked to the second floor, paused in front of the cell. The Black Wolf was alone, a rarity, but he was leaving by himself today.

The Black Wolf sat still on his bunk, his back straight, hands on his knees. He noticed Mosby in his periphery and turned to him. Mosby gave a small nod.

The Black Wolf stood, stretched his back and let out an involuntary groan. He did not stop to look around his cell and he took nothing with him. He stepped out of the open cell door and onto the metal grate platform behind Mosby.

Mosby turned and led the way down the steps.

Word had gotten around. When The Black Wolf appeared on the first floor, chatter stopped. No laughing, no more complaining about a lousy night's sleep. Each step he took was like turning down a volume knob on the cell block.

Mosby swallowed hard. He knew all eyes were on him and his escort. He knew they would all know he was in on it. He knew they all wanted to be there, too, walking out into the sunshine.

The Black Wolf didn't look at any of the cells. He didn't even acknowledge them as existing. He marched straight down the hall, urging Mosby to walk faster. Now that it was this close and had been delayed already, he didn't want to wait a second more.

They reached the end of the first-floor block. A heavy door of bars waited for them. Mosby knew the man on the other side was with them. Without a word, they came to a stop, then in the nearly silent cellblock, the industrial buzz of the door lock being released sounded.

Like a starter's pistol went off, the prisoners came alive. Shouts, screams, pounding on cell doors, bunk beds, cement walls. The walls rattled, the floors shook. Some shouted encouragement, some finally felt brave enough to shout insults. Many were in Spanish. Through it all The Black Wolf remained stoic. He waited and watched the door slide open, one step closer to freedom. It was difficult, but he let Mosby take the first step though and then he followed, leaving the cacophony behind.

Mosby licked sweat off his lip. He hadn't thought about how public this would all be. Everyone would know about it. There would be consequences. He only hoped enough people were paid off to keep him out of trouble. The truth was, neither James Lee who organized this plan, nor The Black Wolf cared at all what happened to the guards on their payroll once he was gone. They fully expected them to get in trouble, to get fired, to get shivved by a prisoner. None of it mattered to them. The guard's usefulness had been realized and they were disposable.

They passed by the guard stand where Rodriguez didn't look up from his desk. He ignored them as they passed as if not acknowledging them would make it not real. Like his part in this break-out was passed over.

The buzzer sounded again as the doors slid shut, sealing the rest of the men inside to live out their sentences.

On the second floor Tito lay on his bunk. He heard the door close and the riled-up noises of the prisoners reacting to his boss merely walking out of the prison. Such a simple plan, he thought, but so effective. A blunt instrument, but James Lee hadn't had enough time to execute the plan he wanted.

Tito knew his protection was gone. His influence was gone. His status was gone.

The organization still had some sway. And when The Black Wolf returned to Mexico and re-installed himself in position, he promised to make sure Tito and the others were cared for. But Tito also knew the realities of life inside. A dozen men or more had been waiting for their chance to make a run at him, but they never could because of The Black Wolf.

Now, when Tito went out into the yard, or down to the mess hall, he would do so with a target on his back. He would be walking into a den of lions with raw meat hanging from his clothes. He wished The Black Wolf well, but also cursed the man for abandoning him.

CHAPTER FORTY-EIGHT

Warden Frank Scalise left his desk and walked to the outer office where his secretary sat. Emmy was filing her nails. She'd come with the job when he took over, and for all he knew, she came with the building as well when it was built. Her white hair was sprayed into place each morning and her fake pearl necklaces clacked and rattled any time she moved. But she kept all his messages straight and reminded him when his anniversary was approaching.

"What's that racket, Emmy?"

She looked up and tilted her head like a dog. The noise from the cell block was little more than a drone up in the office, but it was punctuated by the occasional thump of fifty prisoners banging on cell bars as one.

"I dunno," she said.

Scalise went to the window and checked the yard. Everything looked normal down there. He went to the door and listened. The rumble was still there. Something was going on down on the block.

He hadn't been at work for more than five minutes. No matter how many times he tried to beat Emmy in, he never seemed to. This morning he woke early, determined to figure out if he still wanted the job at all. He would get in early, really take stock of things and try to decide his future. Then there she was at her desk, like she lived below it in some studio apartment built beneath the floorboards. And now this. Who could think about their future with all this racket going on?

Scalise crossed back to his office to call the guard station. Before he could reach the door, one of his guards, Matthews, came through the outer door, breathing hard.

"We got a problem."

Scalise voiced his worst fear. "Riot?"

"Nearly. But there's something else."

Emmy ignored them and kept right on sawing at her fingernails.

* * *

CONCHO PULLED INTO A PARKING LOT OUTSIDE A BIG BOX STORE where he was told to meet the team. Several men and women stood around looking serious, coffee cups in most of their hands. Concho hung his ranger badge off his shirt pocket and went for the man he thought looked in charge.

Agent William Shea wore the trademark navy blue windbreaker with DEA in yellow on the back. He was tall with thick, dark hair that had its share of salt in with the pepper. He gave the air of a career law enforcement man, military background, leadership material in a my-way-or-the-highway style.

He clocked Concho headed his way and thrust his hand out to shake.

"You must be our ranger contact."

"Yes, sir." Concho shook. "Concho Ten-Wolves."

"Ten wolves? That some sort of badass nickname they gave you? Do all Rangers have one of those?"

"Not a nickname, sir. Just my name. Most in my tribe have names like that."

"Tribe?" By his accent, he wasn't from Texas. More like a

Maryland Army brat who was destined to go either DEA or CIA. "You're serious."

"Yes, sir. Kickapoo. Mixed with a little African."

A smile crept up one side of Shea's mouth. "Huh. That's a new one on me." He finally stopped pumping Concho's arm. "I understand you're the one who cracked this thing."

"Yes, sir."

Shea waved him away. "Enough with that sir crap. Call me Bill."

"Okay, Bill." He ran down the quick version of his past week and what led him to The Black Wolf.

Shea pointed to a woman with a tight ponytail and a bullet-proof vest. "This is Vera Lenore from the department of corrections."

He shook her hand. "Pleasure to meet you," he said.

"Likewise," she said.

"We'll have six other agents with us, a warrant, an indict-ment and the full authority of the federal government to cut this guy off and make sure he rots in solitary until his grand-kids go gray."

Concho nodded. "I'm here however you want to use me."

Shea glared at the two Double Eagles on his belt. "I hope we don't have to use you like that."

"Like I say," Concho said. "Any way you need me."

Shea smiled again and shouted to the team. "Let's mount up."

Concho turned back to his pickup truck, thinking that Shea had probably been wanting to use that expression ever since got off the plane in Texas.

* * *

THEY STEPPED OUT INTO THE SUNSHINE. THE SUN WAS STILL low in the east and didn't make it over the wall yet for The Black Wolf to see the yellow ball in the sky, but he felt the heat and saw the world brighter than he ever had in all his times being out in the yard. Only a hundred and fifty feet straight forward to the last gate before the outside.

James Lee checked the tower for the rifleman. He saw him flinch, but then he noticed Mosby with them and he relaxed. The rifleman was not on the payroll.

They walked quickly now, all three of them just wanting it to be over. In the guard booth by the gate sat Simmons. A tall, athletic African American, his face was sour and his attitude the same at having been called in to cover for Garver last-minute. He'd gotten his son off to school, his daily routine. Damn them if they were mad he wasn't there spot on at seven. Since his wife left, he was all Daryl had and he was determined to give that kid a solid structure. That meant being there when he said he would be there. And that meant the job took the back seat to his only son.

Simmons lifted his chin as a greeting to Mosby, then he saw who he had with him. James Lee, he had seen before from all his many visits. That boy came and went more than most of the lawyers for the inmates. But behind him, bringing up the last in line, was The Black Wolf.

Working outside the cell blocks meant there were some guards who had very little interaction with inmates at all. Simmons was one of them. But he knew The Black Wolf. He had seen him in the yard now and then, but he'd never seen him out here. And if he was being released, the whole crew would have been talking about it.

"What's up?" Simmons asked.

"Open up," Mosby said.

"Open up?"

"Yeah. Come on."

Mosby shifted back and forth on his feet, licked sweat off his lip like it was coated in sugar. His eyes wouldn't stay fixed on one spot for more than a second. Simmons smelled trouble.

"What's going on, Mosby?"

"You need to open up. That's what's going on. It's all approved."

The Black Wolf stood still and stoic behind the guard.

"Yeah, come on," James Lee said. "We're running late."

For what, he did not say. But on any con, act like you're meant to be there and they will think you are. If Simmons were smart, he would buzz the gate open and they could all skip the next phase of the plan. The new part.

"I didn't hear anything about this," Simmons said.

"Garver knew about it. Must not have told you."

Simmons was still inside his tiny booth, bulletproof glass between them. He stood from his chair, ignoring the six video monitors with feeds from cameras placed around the perimeter. He knew all the action was right here and right now.

James Lee had approached him about joining the payroll. That was two years ago and he'd told him to go screw himself. The money would have been good, especially for Daryl, but Simmons didn't play like that.

James Lee hadn't mentioned anyone who was taking money, but Simmons suspected now that Mosby was one of them.

Simmons put a hand on the handle of his pistol.

"Let me call upstairs."

"No," Mosby said too fast and too loud. "We're late. You'll get me in trouble."

James Lee knew this wasn't going to happen without the next phase. He stepped up to the window and smiled. "You really need to open that gate. If you don't, you won't like the outcome."

"What's that supposed to mean?" Simmons shot quick glances up toward the tower, hoping the rifleman might look down here and take notice.

"It means you are involved in this whether you want to be or not. And if you don't open that gate, bad things will happen."

"This some sort of bust-out?"

"Some sort. Now, like I said, we're behind schedule. Open the damn gate."

Simmons drew his pistol. "I can't do that."

Mosby looked like he was going to pass out. James Lee looked to him, expecting him to draw his own weapon, but it stayed in the holster.

"Mr. Simmons, this is a mistake."

"Turn around and march him back inside unless you want your head blown off instead. You know we got rifles up top, right?"

"But do you know what I have?"

Simmons scanned him up and down, looking for a weapon. He saw nothing.

"Mosby, I don't know how you got mixed up with this crew, but you need to drop your weapon and back up."

Mosby pleaded with him. "Simmons, please. Believe him."

"Believe him about what?"

"About what I have."

Simmons was in a bind. From behind the bulletproof glass he could do little. If he stepped out of his booth, he opened himself up to attack from what it was that James Lee had.

"You won't get away with it," Simmons said.

James Lee just chuckled. "Leo!"

His voice was loud. Loud enough to travel beyond the gate. Beyond to the street outside, where the four black Navigators were waiting. Where Leo stood as he'd been instructed, holding on to the new part of the plan.

"Daddy?"

Simmons's face fell. It was his son's voice on the other side of the gate.

"So you can see now," James Lee said. "Why it's very important for you to open that gate."

CHAPTER FORTY-NINE

SIMMONS KEPT HIS GUN AIMED AT JAMES LEE THROUGH THE glass as the buzz of the gate release sounded like a drill bit coming closer and closer to his eye. All he had to see was one sneaker and he knew it was Daryl. When the gate parted enough for Simmons to see his son's entire body, he also saw the man with a gun to his head. And he saw the fear in the boy's eyes, the tear-streaked face, the running nose.

"You son of a—"

"All you have to do is nothing," James Lee said. "Once we get in the cars and go, we leave him behind. But no alarm bells, no phone calls. If we could get to him once, we can get to him again, even if we are miles away."

"Mosby, how can you get tied in with this scum?"

"It ain't my fault," Mosby said. His face had become nearly as pained as Daryl's. The regret and pain of his choices on full display.

"We're going to walk now," James Lee said. "You can shoot us, but just know that you do, the kid is dead. If you even look like you're going to take a shot, the kid is dead. You look that way." James Lee pointed back toward the prison. "And you wait until you hear the cars leave and then you close the gate and act like we were never here."

The muscles in Simmons's jaw flexed. He did the math in his head about his chances of shooting all three of them before Daryl would take one in the skull. Not worth the risk.

"Daddy...?"

The single word broke him. Simmons set his gun down on the counter in front of him and turned toward the tan prison walls.

James Lee crooked a finger for The Black Wolf to follow him. Mosby stood still, tears running down his face.

James Lee passed by the kid and into an open door in the backseat of the second Navigator in line.

The Black Wolf stopped for a moment when he was beside Simmons.

"You could have taken the money. Now you keep your life, your son's. Either way, I am a generous man."

He stepped forward and set a palm on the boy's face. "Good boy." He patted him twice and then calmly walked to the open door and got in beside James Lee.

The gunman waited until the door closed. He checked quickly to see if any of the guards were going to act like heroes. When he saw nobody, he shoved Daryl forward.

The boy stumbled and placed his palms on the door to the guard shack to brace himself and keep from falling over. Simmons heard the noise and wanted to turn around but he obeyed his orders and kept staring at the prison wall until he heard the sounds of the cars driving away.

* * *

INSIDE THE DARK INTERIOR OF THE NAVIGATOR, THE BLACK Wolf settled into the most comfortable seat he had been in for nine and three-quarter years. The air was just the temperature he liked. There was a chilled bottle of water in the door handle cup holder.

He placed a hand on James Lee's arm and squeezed.

"Yeah, wait on that," James Lee said. "We still got a long way to go."

A walkie-talkie crackled to life. "All in?"

James Lee lifted it from the pocket in his door and keyed the talk button. "Good to go."

The rumble of four V-8 engines all came to life at once. The car moved forward for a few seconds and then jerked to a halt.

James Lee keyed the button again. "What the hell was that?"

"We got a problem."

* * *

Warden Frank Scalise had come down out of his office. He'd checked in quickly at the cell block where the prisoners still carried on shouting and banging and rattling bars. He got filled in on the break-out.

Who?" he asked.

"Black Wolf."

Scalise made a choice right then and there.

On his way out the side gate, he stopped at the armory. The shotgun he lifted off the wall rack had dust on it. He grabbed a fist full of shells and put them in his pocket, barking orders to the men following him. There were two, only Matthews, who had come to his office to tell him of the trouble, and de Joya.

He'd been hurrying so Scalise hadn't grabbed a walkie.

He went out the side gate leading the way. His tie caught a breeze and blew up in his face. He pushed it back down and stomped quickly along the sidewalk beside the two-story tall outer wall of Bigfoot. When they turned the corner, they saw a man shove a young boy through the gate and then the doors close on a line of four black SUVs.

Scalise stepped off the curb and into the street, lifting the shotgun as he did. He racked in a round and stood with his legs shoulder width apart.

Scalise didn't say anything. He didn't need to. The SUVs stopped.

"Call Wilson," he said to Matthews. Matthews lifted the walkie from his belt and called the sniper in the tower.

"Wilson? Alamo Street. West Gate. Shoot it if it moves."

"Copy," came the reply.

Frank Scalise raised his voice over the rumble of the engines.

"Back inside, Fulgencio!"

He couldn't see anything behind the tinted glass of the SUVs, had no idea which car The Black Wolf was inside. He figured that was part of the plan. Scalise waited for whatever came next, but he knew no matter what it was, he was standing his ground at last.

* * *

JAMES LEE PUNCHED THE BACK OF THE SEAT IN FRONT OF HIM. "Damn it, damn it, damn it."

He keyed his walkie. "Get us out of here. Now."

The passenger window of the front SUV rolled down with a slight whir of the automatic motor. Wallace and de Joya braced, handguns in their two-handed grips ready to fire.

A hand came out of the window holding a 9mm and opened fire. At the same time an AR-15 opened fire from the back seat window, and from the second SUV in line, another AR-15 opened up out of the front passenger window.

Scalise started firing. Buckshot sprayed the front grille and windshield of the lead SUV. Williams and de Joya each ran for cover while firing. Williams was the first to take a hit. A line of bullets from an AR-15 stitched across his chest and he went down.

From up in the tower, Wilson began shooting with his rifle.

Simmons didn't wait for the car engine noises anymore. He

punched the button to close the gate and pulled his son inside the tiny guard shack and pushed him to the floor for cover.

The street came alive with bullets. Scalise fired and pumped, fired and pumped. A shot from the 9mm hit his thigh. He bent forward and another shot entered the top of his skull. He was dead before his face hit the pavement.

de Joya fell in a hail of AR-15 shots.

Wilson's rifle shots pierced bodywork and shattered glass, but did nothing to stop the SUVs when they all seemed to lurch forward at once and squealed tires, speeding away down the street.

In less than thirty seconds the sounds of engines died down, the echoes of bullets fired faded away. There was only the low wind and the sound of Scalise's tie flapping in the breeze.

CHAPTER FIFTY

CONCHO DROVE UP TO A SCENE LIKE A WAR ZONE AFTER THE battle had ended. Three bodies lay in the street. Broken glass sparkled in the morning sun. He recognized the body of Warden Scalise and he sighed a weary breath.

The two other vehicles that arrived with Concho, black government-owned SUVs just like the ones The Black Wolf escaped in, disgorged agents and the street was quickly filled with people. Guns were drawn, perimeters checked, but The Black Wolf and his accomplices were gone.

William Shea took charge, barking orders and pointing people in different directions, but there was nothing to be done here. Later, the surveillance cameras would fill in the blanks, but between Simmons in the booth and Wilson in the tower they would have a full accounting of what went down.

While the other agents checked the gate, peered around corners and examined the dead bodies, Concho looked up. Wilson stood in his tower looking down on them, the rifle in the crook of his elbow. Concho shielded his eyes from the sun and Wilson stared straight at him. Without a word, Wilson pointed south. Concho gave him a quick nod.

"They went that way," Concho said. He started walking toward his truck.

"What?" said Shea. "How do you know?"

Concho didn't stop moving, he made Shea follow him. "First, look at the tire mark there." He pointed down to where two fresh skid marks started thick and then faded out facing south. "Second," he said and pointed up to the tower. "They saw them."

Shea followed his finger and saw Wilson with his arm facing south like a weather vane in a high wind.

Shea swirled in his hand over his head. "Mount up! They went south!"

Concho was in his truck and in drive before the others could get inside their fancy government SUVs.

* * *

A STEADY HISS CAME FROM UNDER THE HOOD OF THE LEAD Navigator. A small geyser of steam spouted from a hole in the hood made from a rifle round. The driver keyed his walkie.

"My engine's dying."

James Lee cursed and lifted his walkie-talkie. "How bad?"

"I ain't gonna make it to Mexico, that's for damn sure."

James Lee heard a loud pop through the walkie and the SUV they rode in slowed. He leaned his head to look out the window and see the lead SUV drift over the the curb and come to a stop.

"Damn it."

The Black Wolf put a hand on James Lee's shoulder and he went cold. He turned to face the boss in the tight confines of the back seat.

"I'm out," said The Black Wolf, "But I'm not yet free."

"I know. It's no problem. This is why we have four vehicles. It's all planned. Don't worry."

"I never worry. That's why I pay you."

James Lee pulled open the door. Light flooded the dark

inside of the vehicle. *And you're gonna pay BIG*, thought James Lee as he slammed the door.

The driver of the lead SUV was already out and under the hood.

"Ditch it," James Lee said. "Get hid and come meet us later. Can you get this thing off the main road at least?"

"Nah, she's quit." He slammed the hood. "Won't go an inch." He pointed to three bullet holes in the hood. "He got her real good."

"All right. You're done then. Ditch it and I'll see you down there. Stay out of sight."

"Copy."

James Lee walked fast back to his vehicle, waving his hand to his driver to keep it moving.

* * *

CONCHO RARELY WISHED HE DROVE A BLACK AND WHITE POLICE cruiser, but some light bars and a siren would have helped right then. A dual escort of DEA and Department of Corrections would have to do.

He knew The Black Wolf was only minutes ahead. When they stood on the street outside the walls of Bigfoot, the blood still oozed slowly from beneath the bodies, filling cracks in the pavement. It hadn't even had time to dry in the sun. They were close.

His cell phone rang. Concho pressed the button and he spoke through the F-150's speaker system.

"Yeah?"

Agent William Shea answered back. "You're moving like you know where they're going?"

"He's headed home."

"Home, what? Like, Mexico?"

"Yes. It's gotta be."

I just got off with highway patrol. They have a BOLO out

for black SUVs, which is what I got from the only guy I could raise at the prison. Apparently they shot the warden."

"Yeah, I know. You realize you're driving black SUVs, right?"

"If highway patrol pulls us over, I'll explain their mistake. I told them to get a bird in the air, too."

Concho barely slowed for a stop sign, then gassed the engine again, headed for Highway Fifty-Five. "Something must have gone wrong. No way they wanted to leave with that much noise."

"Maybe the warden died trying to be a hero."

"Just watch out. If they're running scared, they're dangerous."

"Yeah, I kinda got that from the bodies all over the damn street."

"More dangerous than usual," Concho clarified.

Shea spoke with all confidence. "No way they're making the border. Not on my watch."

Concho had been thinking it but didn't dare say it out loud.

They hung up, promising to stay in touch, even though Concho could see them in his rearview mirrors. But the more time that passed and the more miles under his tires, the more he questioned if he'd guessed wrong on their destination.

* * *

The Black Wolf's silence annoyed James Lee. So far, there had been no thank you. No, "good job." No appreciation at all. The longer he sat next to the man, the more he realized he'd never spent any time with him outside the prison. He'd seen him in a cell, in the visitor's room, in the yard, but that was it. Now that he was out, The Black Wolf acted even more entitled. Even more like he was in charge of the world at large and not just his tiny little sliver of it.

James Lee couldn't wait to be rid of this burden.

They came to Uvalde and turned onto Highway Eighty-Three South. Getting closer.

The landscape seemed to drain of what little green there had been. All browns and hard plants that looked like each day was a fight for survival. This was the land of armadillos clad in armor, tortoises with their hard shells, snakes in their skin tough enough to make boots out of. You needed thick skin to live here.

James Lee sat back and dreamed of sand and the Caribbean Ocean.

His walkie-talkie crackled to life.

"Heads up."

James Lee replied. The Black Wolf sat still next to him, not doing a damn thing for his own escape plan. "What's up?"

"State trooper."

"Did he clock you?"

"Not sure."

"Keep an eye on it."

James Lee felt the cold stare of The Black Wolf in the seat next to him.

"There is a plan for this?" The Black Wolf asked.

"Yes," James Lee replied. "There's a plan for everything."

* * *

"Spotted 'em leaving Uvalde."

Concho could hear the satisfied grin on Shea's face even over the speaker. They were midway through Uvalde themselves.

"Headed onto eighty-three?"

"Yeah, looks like."

"Definitely going for the border."

"Worse comes to worse, that's where they'll nail 'em." Shea had started to adopt a put-on Texas accent. Too much time among the locals.

"They'll have a spot far away from the crossing at Eagle

Pass. Some coyote trail, they'll have backup. Someone to meet them just across the border with a vehicle. Maybe a plane. They planned this. They have contingencies."

"Then we get them before they make it that far."

Concho pushed the truck a little faster.

CHAPTER FIFTY-ONE

THEY CAUGHT SIGHT OF THE TRAIN OF THREE SUVs JUST north of the Nueces River. By then they had picked up two state patrol cars to add to their convoy. Concho still had the lead.

He figured there would be no way at all that The Black Wolf could escape, but he also knew better than to underestimate a man who had the resources to break out of Bigfoot and to continually run a criminal organization from behind bars.

A call came in from Shea. Concho had been waiting for this one, the takeover. The big-shot DEA agent telling Concho to stand down while he takes lead at the last moment so he can get the glory of busting the notorious Black Wolf.

"What's the plan, Concho?" Shea asked.

Concho was surprised. It took him a moment to think.

"We know they're armed and desperate. I don't think full frontal assault is the way to go."

"Agreed."

"Can highway patrol set up a roadblock?"

"Already on it."

"Then we stay in sight of them until we hit that. Then we

have them boxed in. All goes well, they see how futile it is and give up."

"Just for the record," Shea said. "I'm authorized at a federal level for lethal force."

"Good to know."

"I'll check in when we get close to the block."

"Copy that."

No sooner had they hung up than Concho saw brake lights. The line of SUVs in front of him was slowing down.

THEY NEEDED A CROSSROADS. UP AHEAD, PRIOR TO THE BRIDGE across the Nueces River, there were rural access roads on either side. James Lee ordered the cars to stop.

They knew the police were behind them. They knew they would be up ahead, too. It hadn't gone well. Too rushed. Too many tiny last-second changes. Maybe it never would have worked. Maybe it never should have. The more James Lee looked at the stone face of the man next to him, the more he thought this was a man who should live out his days behind bars.

The line of cars behind them also slowed and stopped. The two state troopers had lights running. One of the black SUVs had a dash-mounted blue light spinning. No sirens, only the constant wind rolling over the flat Texas scrub.

James Lee keyed his walkie. "Okay, Chris, you go right, Leon, you go left. We'll see you at the meet. However you need to do it to get away, you do it."

"Copy."

"Copy."

"On my go," James Lee said, then set down the walkie.

The Black Wolf ran a hand down over his face. He looked tired now.

"This is not what I was promised."

"We were rushed," James Lee said.

"That is an excuse."

His anger was too close to the surface to be contained. "Of course it's an excuse. What else do you want from me?"

"My freedom. Like I was promised." The Black Wolf leaned closer. "Like I paid for."

"Maybe that's the problem," James Lee said. "You pay for things but you don't actually *do* anything. When was the last time you did something for yourself? You have people who break legs for you, who kill for you, who collect money for you, who sell drugs for you. What do *you* do? You do so little, you were able to still do it from inside a prison cell."

The Black Wolf stared back at James Lee. He remained calm though a dark storm brewed behind his eyes. James Lee, on the other hand, was through holding back. His face turned red, spit flew from his lips like grease in a pan full of bacon.

"You just use everyone around you to make your life easier. And you complain. All you do is complain. All while living a life behind bars that is better than ninety percent of the people I know on the outside. You're lazy, you're fat and I'm done. I'm done working for someone who doesn't do anything."

James Lee pulled the gun from his belt and handed it to The Black Wolf.

"You wanna get out there and shoot it out? Go ahead. You want to run this little escape operation? Go ahead! Just do something."

The Black Wolf hefted the gun in his hand twice. He looked out the window at the waiting row of cars filled with people eager to drag him back to prison.

"You think I am weak because I have people to do things for me."

James Lee had said his piece. He stared back at his boss, face still red.

"You think I have lost touch with what it is to be a soldier. But you don't know me. You don't know that I've done enough and seen enough to last me ten lifetimes. That I earned my rest. I earned my respect. You are the one who is weak because you take orders from a man you don't respect."

The gun bucked. James Lee grunted and his hand went to cover the wound. The Black Wolf fired again and the shot went through James Lee's hand and into his gut.

The Black Wolf reached past him and opened the door. He put a foot up and kicked James Lee out. His body hit the pavement and he squirmed to his right. The Black Wolf fired once more and James Lee lay still. He pulled the door closed.

"Drive."

CHAPTER FIFTY-TWO

Up ahead, the three SUVs split apart like a squad of wide receivers on a well-rehearsed play. One cut east, another west along the access roads, and the Navigator that had just dumped a body on the road roared off south.

The SUVs headed east and west both erupted in automatic weapon fire. Windows were rolled down and AR-15s stuck out spitting lead. Concho saw a flash of his time in Afghanistan. Fast-escaping cars shooting indiscriminately at anyone in a military vehicle.

From behind him, the DEA vehicle growled to life and spun tires around him. It chased the vehicle moving west, letting loose with return fire from handguns.

Behind them, the SUV with the corrections officers chased the Navigator headed east.

He had to admire them, running at the danger instead of away from it, but he knew they were wrong. Those two were bait, and they took it like bass in a lake, mouths open dumbly as they went after the shiniest lure. The vehicle that had dumped a body intrigued Concho. It didn't lay down any cover fire. It simply drove off. But whoever was inside was ruthless enough to kill one of their own and toss his body out like a food wrapper. Only one man was that cold-blooded—The Black Wolf.

The two state troopers divided up and each went with one of the SUVs on the chase. Almost immediately, the DEA vehicle took a long row of hits that raked across the hood and down into the wheel wells and obliterated the right front tire. The heavy vehicle dug into the ground and skidded to a halt.

Concho laid down a streak of rubber as he took off after the southbound Navigator. He juked left to avoid the rumpled pile of James Lee Morris left bleeding in the road.

They crossed up and over the bridge. The river below was lower than normal. It had been a dry year and the brown landscape showed it.

Concho closed the gap they'd been letting sit between them. He got within two car lengths before any shooting started. From the passenger seat up front, Concho's truck was near impossible to hit. They mostly meant it as a warning. Concho tucked the F-150 to the left behind the Navigator. Unless the driver wanted to shoot and drive at the same time, he was safe here.

He waited for his chance at a pit maneuver. He hadn't heard if there would be a helicopter assisting them or not. From the looks of it, he was on his own. Texas highways have a way of making you feel that way. All he had to do now was wait for his moment and hope he'd picked the right car.

*   *   *

James Lee's words still stung like the lingering pain of a slap to the face. The Black Wolf *did* things. Being in charge isn't about pulling triggers and cracking skulls. He had his time with that when he was coming up. It's how he got where he was. That ex-guard didn't know a damn thing about him.

To prove it—to whom? A dead man left back on the road? —The Black Wolf powered down his window and hefted the gun in his hand.

* * *

A BULLET CLIPPED HIS SIDE MIRROR, AND CONCHO JERKED THE wheel by instinct. He skidded and slowed, disappointed in himself at his overreaction. He knew he could pull one of the Double Eagles and shoot back, but left-handed out the window of a moving truck? He'd sooner hit a bird flying overhead than the vehicle in front of him. He didn't want to wait any longer.

Concho accelerated and eyeballed the right rear bumper of the Navigator. Shots rang out, and three bullets whizzed past him. He saw the arm retract back through the window, and he knew he had his moment. Reloading. He had only seconds.

He pressed the gas all the way to the floor and brought the front bumper of his truck up to the back bumper of the Navigator and watched the gap close.

Not yet, not yet, not yet…now!

Concho jerked the wheel left, his bumper clipped the back of the SUV and it began to spin. Concho braked and watched as the driver tried to steer back in a straight line. The massive vehicle swung across both lanes. The driver turned into the swerve but went too far with it. Two wheels came off the ground before they slammed back down and the rubber bit and spun the SUV off to the left again.

The whole body leaned in a slow roll until the front tires went off the road. Then it happened all at once. Still at seventy miles an hour, the front caught in the dirt and the SUV was spinning like a pig on a spit. Concho counted three, four, five rotations before the ground slowed it enough that it merely slid along the dirt at a ninety-degree angle, the passenger doors scraping along the earth.

Concho slowed and pulled to the side. He got out and drew both Colt Double Eagles.

A scar had been dug into the land and the vehicle hissed and ticked like a creature in its death throes. Broken glass scattered the dirt all around it and the wheels still spun.

Concho approached with caution. He circled from the back

to the front, passing the underside of the vehicle with its leaking fluids and bent axles. He reached the front and paused, peering through the front windshield from an angle.

The safety glass was cracked, but he could see the driver wrestling with his seatbelt. The passenger was not moving. Concho stepped out in view of the windshield.

"Texas Ranger, hands where I can see them."

The driver took a moment to register what he was seeing. He was clearly stunned and probably concussed from the accident. He hesitated, then reached down for his sidearm. Concho fired. Both hands gave two rounds each.

The glass fully shattered, soaking the inside of the cab with a rain of glass pellets. The driver was motionless, still belted in place and gravity tugging his body to the right, his arms limp and pointing to the ground, his hair sloped to one side. The passenger hadn't moved or flinched at the sound of the shots, so Concho knew he was gone. Now to the back seat.

Concho side-stepped past the front of the Navigator and was thinking how he would reach the door now on top of the car as it sat on its side when he noticed footsteps in the sand and heard the sound of heavy breathing and footfalls.

The sunroof was open, the glass shattered. He turned toward the desert to see the figure of a man limping away in an attempt to run. The Black Wolf at last.

CHAPTER FIFTY-THREE

"Texas Ranger, freeze!"

The Black Wolf was a good hundred yards ahead of him but moving slowly. Concho knew verbal commands were pointless. He trotted after him, tucking one gun into his holster. The ground was dry and uneven, scattered with brown bushes little more than sticks, a few cacti, rocks and sand that was gritty and thick.

He tried to look ahead and see if The Black Wolf was armed, but he didn't see anything in his hands. Soon, he had closed the gap and now stood only twenty feet behind his prey.

"Stop," he commanded. The Black Wolf limped on.

It would be easy to shoot him out here. Be done with it. He deserved it, for all he'd done. But he was unarmed, his back to Concho. Not his way.

"I said stop."

The Black Wolf stumbled, he tried to catch himself but he fell face first next to a small cluster of rock. Concho ran to him.

He heard The Black Wolf making quick noises of pain with each heavy breath in. At first he thought he must have twisted an ankle or even broken something. Then he heard another sound above the whining complaints. A rattle. He saw movement and turned in time to see the diamond pattern slither away as the snake took shelter again, angry at being disturbed the first time.

Concho turned back to The Black Wolf and saw him clutching at his leg just above the ankle. He kept his gun drawn while he bent to examine him.

"Quit your whining," Concho said.

He peeled The Black Wolf's hand off his leg. He could see the two red dots where the fangs had sunk in. He knew how far they were from help, how difficult it would be to carry him back to the truck and how unlikely it would be to get him anywhere in time to do much for him. At the very best, he would lose the leg.

Concho holstered his gun.

"Freedom," he said. "Isn't all it's cracked up to be, is it?"

Concho turned and walked back to his truck.

CHAPTER FIFTY-FOUR

ALL HE WANTED TO DO WAS SIT AND READ IN THE QUIET. HE bent open the spine on a new Joe Lansdale book, a real Texas writer. He knew little about the book, but he knew Joe always entertained him.

His phone rang. Dalton Shaw. Concho slid a bookmark in and closed the book.

"Yes, Chief?"

"Sorry to bother you, Concho. I know I said I'd give you a few days, but this jerk from the DEA is on my ass for a statement."

"Shea?"

"Yeah, that's the one. Working a fake Texas accent like it's supposed to get me on his side or something. All I know is if it wasn't for you out there, The Black Wolf would be back in ol' Mexico by now. Can you spare an hour this afternoon to give a statement and get him out of our hair?"

"Sure, chief."

They arranged a time. Concho knew William Shea would probably offer him a job again, like he did in the field when Concho returned to where his broken down SUV lay in the sand and told him The Black Wolf was dead. Concho politely declined him then and he would do it again.

He stood, stretching out his back and feeling the past few days' stress and struggles in his muscles.

Maria poked her head in from the other room.

"You going somewhere? Thought you were reading?"

"Gotta go in and talk to the DEA guys."

"I was leaving you alone," she said, sliding her body into the room. She wore tight cutoff jean shorts, a tank top, a sly smile. "I know to leave you to it when you're reading."

"Thank you."

"You leaving now?"

"In about an hour."

"Oh, that's just enough time, then."

Maria took the Lansdale book from his hand and set it down, then leaned up and kissed him hard, pulling him close to her so tight he lost his breath.

"Good to have you home," she said.

"Good to be home."

They kissed again.

"Only an hour, huh?" she said.

"I can be late."

Concho Ten-Wolves scooped her into his arms and carried her to bed.

A LOOK AT BOOK NINE:
BORDER BLOOD

**SADDLE UP FOR A WILD RIDE IN THE NINTH
INSTALLMENT OF THE HEART-STOPPING AND
ADVENTUROUS CONCHO SERIES.**

Stripped of his police powers as a result of an ongoing investigation
involving a shooting on the border, Texas Ranger Concho Ten-Wolves
reluctantly becomes embroiled in the search for a missing young
Indian girl.

But his world takes a riveting twist with the sudden reemergence of a
figure from his troubled youth spent on the Rez—Indian movie star,
Vince Hawk.

As Concho delves deeper into the hunt for the missing girl, the
shadows of the Rez and his enigmatic history with Hawk resurface,
and the stakes grow higher as a sinister turn in the investigation brings
a ruthless gang of killers hell-bent on his destruction.

AVAILABLE FEBRUARY 2024

ABOUT THE AUTHOR

Called the "New Maestro of Noir" by Ken Bruen, Eric Beetner is the author of over twenty-five novels of crime, mystery and suspense—described by Paul Bishop as "the standard by which all current hardboiled and noir writers should be judged."

Beetner has been nominated for an ITW award, a Shamus award, a Derringer award, and three Anthony awards. He hosted the podcast *Writer Types* for more than one hundred episodes and has been host of *Noir at the Bar L.A.* for more than a decade.

For more information, visit ericbeetner.com.

Made in the USA
Coppell, TX
03 October 2024

38114395R00144